D1579691

A definitive chronicle of the
human race, comprising a
retrospective and comparative
look at mankind's triumphs and
follies throughout the ages.
Honest.

THE LOG:

A Dwarfer's Guide to Everything

CRAIG CHARLES

PENGUIN BOOKS

PENGUIN BOOKS

Published by the Penguin Group
Penguin Books Ltd, 27 Wrights Lane, London W8 5TZ, England
Penguin Putnam Inc., 375 Hudson Street, New York, New York 10014, USA
Penguin Books Australia Ltd, Ringwood, Victoria, Australia
Penguin Books Canada Ltd, 10 Alcorn Avenue, Toronto, Ontario, Canada M4V 3B2
Penguin Books (NZ) Ltd, 182–190 Wairau Road, Auckland 10, New Zealand

Penguin Books Ltd, Registered Offices: Harmondsworth, Middlesex, England

First published in Great Britain 1997
10 9 8 7 5 4 3 2 1

Filmset in 10/15pt Eurostyle

Printed in England by Clays Ltd, St Ives plc

CONTENTS

INTRODUCTION

(A rambling, spurious attempt to justify the existence of this book)

Episodes of *Red Dwarf* tend to focus on the more exciting and noteworthy events in the life of the crew. However, it's not all thrills and spills for the characters or the actors. Many hours are spent slumped around the set while the crew strive to mend the carefully crafted props that, for some reason, seem to fall apart in my hands as soon as the director says 'Action'. During these periods of relative calm, I sometimes wonder what my character would do in the quiet, untroubled times between adventures.

Lister would probably spend many hours alone in his bunk, pondering the ramifications of being the only surviving example of *Homo sapiens* in the universe.

Personally, I tend to pass the time on set arguing with Danny about music or winding Robert up about how middle-class he is. But what if I really were the last remaining human? How would I fill that endless chasm between sleep and curry, knowing that I was the last example of, and final spokesman for, an occasionally great race? I'd like to think the last human would spend his time compiling a comparative list of scientific and sociological milestones in the development of the human race. An attempt, if you will, to leave something for posterity. Something that says 'When I'm gone, the human race will be no more, but my people were once noble and clever and, look, we even invented the whoopee cushion.' Of course, Dave Lister isn't the first name that springs to mind as the ideal chronicler of the human race, and neither is Craig Charles. However, if you're the last human being in the universe it's a little hard to delegate.

'But!', I hear you cry, 'surely Dave Lister is merely a character in a TV series'. Yes, but, in an infinite universe, if something CAN exist, then it MUST exist. Therefore Dave is out there somewhere, and I'd like to think a little bit of me is with him, hopefully not the bit he keeps in his undergarments.

Nostradamus made numerous predictions about the future. He foretold the death of kings, the coming of comets and even the arrival of an individual named Hister (sound familiar?), who would have a marked effect on human history. Not unlike Nostradamus, I have taken the liberty of predicting certain developments in man's future. To do this I have used a literary trick known in the trade as 'Making it up'. If you've just bought this book at an antiquarian bookfair on Betelgeuse and you notice that some of my predictions are a tad off the mark, well, that's just tough. I'll have been dead for two hundred years so what you think is the least of my problems.

If, however, you've bought this book new (thank you,

I'll always love you), allow me to reassure you that everything in this book has been carefully researched, cross-referenced, annotated, then thrown away and made up from scratch while at least partially drunk, which is probably the best state to be in when you read it.

If the last remaining human being in the universe left behind a book of any kind, I suspect it wouldn't be entirely dissimilar to the tome you are now holding. Ladies and gentlemen, I give you, THE LOG. I hope you enjoy it as much as I enjoyed one afternoon last summer with two synchronized swimmers and a bucket of strawberry mousse.

PART ONE

THE
DEVELOPMENT
OF THE HUMAN RACE

In a break from tradition, the first part of this log takes up more than half the book. However, I feel this is more than justified given the subject matter which is, in fact, 'Everything'.

'But', being a pedantic git, you might say: 'If the first part deals with everything, what on earth is the rest of the book about?' I would have thought that was obvious: 'Everything else' of course. If you have trouble with this concept you have either bought the wrong book, or, you've been standing in a bookshop so long reading it that you are now surrounded by a posse of Ninja-Book-Shop-Sales-Persons who will kill you horribly if you don't buy this publication for cash and order the sequel on credit.

The later parts of the book consist of thoughts, recipes, personal observations and little collections of accumulated wisdom garnered over many years of enthu-siastic wisdom-garnering. If I were the last remaining human, I would include these sections in my log because, they say, you should write about what you know, and frankly, I don't know anything else.

Primitive man developed a simple system of counting that consisted of 'one, two, many'. As tribal communities evolved, this system became inefficient. If a scout returned with news of 'Many' enemies coming over the hill, the chief didn't know if he meant three guys with a catapult or twenty-four thousand nutcases armed with big sticks. This led to a more sophisticated system of counting that introduced the concept of 'Shitloads'. This word became a cue to run away very fast and hide in a bush.

Counting became important in other aspects of life in the ancient world. Kings would be frustrated at not knowing how many wives they had. They might know they had 'Shitloads', but if they didn't know exactly how many, how could they keep track of them all? Thus were accountants born.

Later on in Man's evolution, mathematics was developed into an exact science by such luminaries as Aristotle, Euclid, Newton, Napier and Einstein. However ...

... in the latter half of the twentieth century, politicians invented a branch of statistics called 'Bollocks', a mathematical method enabling them to prove that anything equalled anything else given adequate funding. This put mathematics back forty-eight thousand years.

The binary system was one of the most important developments of the twentieth century. This stroke of mathematical genius allowed the world to be defined in terms of one or nothing, a counting system that was infinitely less sophisticated than the 'one, two, many' of our prehistoric ancestors. The binary system was developed because, although computers can count really, really fast, they are so stupid they can only count as far as one before they get hopelessly confused and add six noughts to your gas bill.

Chaos Mathematics came to the fore towards the end of the second millennium and was something to do with butterfly wings and water drips but the academic drips that came up with it finally admitted that there was no room in mathematics for damp lepidoptera and began work on something more useful.

In the middle of the twentieth century, mathematics finally reached its nadir when some bright spark called Patek Ramflampanjamram invented a numbering system consisting entirely of zeros. Thereafter, if you asked a computer what it was thinking about, the response was invariably 'Oh, nothing'.

Medicine

In Neolithic times, hunter-gatherers would go forth into the unknown with wooden clubs (or pointed sticks if they were particularly intellectual), and bring back food for their mates and off-spring. However, around this time, a new kind of human also evolved: one that had seen all too clearly what can happen if you confront a hungry sabre-toothed tiger with nothing but a pointy stick and a big mouth; an individual who witnessed a bleeding hunter being dragged back to the cave with a broken stick and a hopelessly overblown story about how he'd almost had the bastard before he got his leg bitten off. This individual rushed forward, and, a voice laden with authority and conviction bellowed 'Let me through, I've got some bones and a rattle!' Thus was modern medicine born.

Early ailments such as headaches, rheumat-ism and sprained ankles were treated by drilling a hole in the head of the afflicted to let the devils out. This didn't cure anything but people tended to complain less about their health, which helped to relieve the burden on their overworked health service. Later on, shamans came to realize that plants could be used to cure certain ailments and they would feed their gullible patients all sorts of rubbishy old roots and weeds until something worked. The ones that didn't die were pronounced cured. Thus was the pharmaceutical industry born and lard was touted as the ultimate food supplement to ensure a long and happy life. Later, Alexander Fleming hit upon the inspired idea of feeding sick people mouldy bread to see what happened. Amazingly, it cured them. It just goes to show, you never know when a weird idea might work.

Over the ages, medicine gradually developed into a thriving science. The shaman's son would take over the family business as, in later years, Harley Street specialists would hand over practices to their equally greedy and pompous offspring. This time-honoured tradition ensured that there would always be someone around who could convince you you'd die without a ten-grand appendix transplant.

The late twentieth century saw the beginnings of genetic engineering as a tool for doing all sorts of weird stuff. This was immediately banned and research in this field ceased everywhere apart from those laboratories that had a lock on the door.

Vitamins were touted as the ultimate supplement to ensure a long and happy life. In 2036 a drug called NeoProzak was made compulsory for everyone on the planet so they didn't get depressed about the ozone layer and afternoon TV scheduling. Rebel enclaves who refused to take it sprung up around the world and they would hide in caves and be miserable and occasionally hit each other on the head with sticks.

Cloning became a popular trend in 2055. Rich people would have a clone of themselves made so they would always have a ready supply of compatible organs when theirs gave out. The clones weren't exactly overjoyed with this concept and in 2060 they formed a union to defend their rights. Sadly, a test case in Arkansas, presided over by a number of rich judges with clones of their own, determined that the clones were the property of the original DNA donors. This led to the clone riots of 2061 in which a number of people ended up beating themselves to death.

2217 saw the invention of an antibiotic so powerful that you had to be in perfect health to take it.

Later, a neo-drug called Infinitol was touted as the key to immortality. It was guaranteed to completely halt the ageing process, a promise it fulfilled to a limited extent in that it invariably killed anyone stupid enough to swallow one.

Clothes were initially invented during the Ice Age when one bright spark theorized that, instead of throwing animal skins away because you couldn't eat them, you could wrap yourself in them and not be so bloody freezing. From that moment on, fashion was invented. Certain skins became *de rigueur* and anyone seen wearing last season's mammoth hide was humiliated with taunts, and left out on the ice to perish until he got stylish or dead, whichever came first. Hemlines rose and fell with the seasons and accessories such as bones and the ears of enemies became the 'in' thing. Leather remained the fabric of choice for about forty thousand years until a very confused person came up with the concept of weaving and the fashion-garment industry really took off. Via a judicious study of worms' bottoms, silk was discovered in the Far East and suddenly women around the globe knew exactly what they wanted for their birthdays. Thus haute couture was born, and from Peking to Timbuktoo, men became poor overnight. The concept of power dressing was instigated in Japan by the Samurai, whose finely crafted garb invariably included a three-foot, razor-sharp head remover. That's power in anyone's language.

Throughout the Orient style and quality reigned. Status was defined by the intricately woven garments worn by the rich and powerful. In Rome and Athens, flowing togas and ornate armour were very much the thing. In Britain, guys painted themselves blue and shouted a lot, thus pre-empting Chelsea supporters by a couple of millennia.

Towards the end of the twentieth century, female fashion was largely defined by skirt length. By the year 2000 skirts had become so short that they were worn round the neck-like chokers and offered little or no protection against the elements, but men were very happy, except during the period when fashion required THEM to wear paisley nappies. Sadly, whichever way they looked at this garment, they couldn't convince themselves it looked good, but at least they were fashionable and, at the end of the day, that's all that mattered.

Possibly the greatest fashion breakthrough occurred in 2198 with the invention of 'Soft' clothes. These were computer-generated clothes that were projected around the body from a digital necklace. Thermal insulation was provided by a variable, kinetic force field that agitated air molecules adjacent to the body to provide heat. The opacity of the virtual garment could be controlled by a small, hand-held unit and much fun was had by teenagers who managed to hack the code for a girl's garment and render it transparent while she was bending over. Girls had equal fun by making guys' clothing transparent while they were looking at the girl bending over, and many a beau was to be seen scurrying for the shadows with his tail between his legs.

For six months in 2210 fashion dictated that clothes should be abandoned altogether in favour of a genetically induced hairy fleece that could be grown to order around the body. This fashion died out quite rapidly when everyone realized that it looked completely gross (although it retained a certain popularity in Greece and Italy where no one noticed the difference).

Historical Footnote

The only recorded instance of a major conflict caused by differing views on fashion was the Tie Wars of the twenty-second century. The workers of the world rebelled against the tie-wearing classes and a bloody conflict ensued. The blue-collar 'Blisters' and the management 'Ties' fought tooth and nail until the Ties introduced a devastating weapon: the Smart But Casual Bomb which would shower the enemy with paisley cravats and hand-tailored lounge suits. The Blisters were about to admit defeat when they suddenly realized that it was they who were manufacturing all the weapons for the Ties, so they stopped. This proved the most decisive strike of the war and the whole thing ended in compromise. The Blisters agreed to do up the top button of their shirts as a concession towards smartness, while the Ties retained their ties but wore them with their top buttons undone as a gesture of solidarity with the workers.

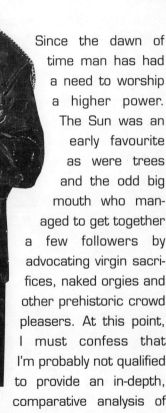

Since the dawn of time man has had a need to worship a higher power. The Sun was an early favourite as were trees and the odd big mouth who managed to get together a few followers by advocating virgin sacrifices, naked orgies and other prehistoric crowd pleasers. At this point, I must confess that I'm probably not qualified to provide an in-depth, comparative analysis of world religions, mainly because I know smeg-all about them. However, I know a lot about smeg. So, here is a précis of the world's religions in terms of smeg:

TAOISM – Smeg happens.

HARE KRISHNA – Smeg happens Rama Rama Hare Hare.

ZEN – What is the sound of smeg clapping?

ISLAM – If smeg happens, take a hostage.

BUDDHISM – When smeg happens, is it really smeg?

JUDAISM – Why does smeg always happen to me?

PROTESTANTISM – Smeg won't happen if I work harder.

CATHOLICISM – If smeg happens, I deserve it.

HINDUISM – This smeg has happened before.

JEHOVAH'S WITNESSES – Knock, knock, 'Smeg happens'.

BAPTISTS – If you go right under, all that smeg will wash off.

UNITARIAN – What's all this smeg about?

SEVENTH DAY ADVENTIST – Smeg happens on Saturdays.

CONFUCIANISM – Confucius, he say 'Smeg happens'.

MORMON – Smeg happens over and over again.

SCIENTOLOGY – The machine says you're full of smeg.

NEW AGE – Smeg comes in spaceships. Let us surround this smeg in white light and heal it.

ROSICRUCIANS – There's a lot of secret smeg you know nothing about.

RASTAFARIANISM – Hey, man, let's smoke some of this smeg.

Well, there you have it. If there are any present-day religions I have failed to include, I'm sorry, I'm not infallible. Also, if I have offended anyone, please forgive me, for I know not what I do.

As with anything in the sphere of human development, religions are constantly evolving and changing. However, all the world's religions were forced to have a bit of a rethink when God turned up in New York on 25 December 2235 and announced His displeasure at the fact that no one had even sent Him a card let alone bought Him a present. Then, when He saw the state His creation was in, He totally lost it and went off in a divine huff saying He never wanted to speak to us again. To be fair, you can't really blame Him.

No one knows exactly when mankind first discovered the concept of humour. I suspect it could have been immediately after a massive carnivore snatched up a hunter, and the hunter's friend, at first stunned by the incident, suddenly burst into fits of uncontrollable laughter. Not so much because his friend's legs looked so funny sticking out of the beast's mouth, but because it wasn't HIM sticking out of the beast's mouth. Also, he could forget about the two tusks and a spear he owed his friend and pop back to the cave and comfort the poor guy's rather attractive mate. How the tears of mirth must have flowed down his grimy prehistoric face and made his beard soggy.

Basically, the vast majority of things that make humans laugh involve something nasty happening to someone that isn't you. German is the only language I know that has a word for this: *schadenfreude*. For some reason, I don't find this surprising.

Sigmund Freud, the father-figure of modern psycho-analysis, wrote a learned tome that analysed and dissected every aspect of what makes us laugh. The book was called *Freud on Humour* and if you want a good laugh, don't read it. When Freud asked 'Why did the chicken cross the road?', it was because he wanted to understand its motivation and cure it of its obsessive desire to cross roads via an in-depth study of its early experiences in the egg.

It is said that there are only five basic jokes, from which all other gags are derived. I can't remember what they are, but if you go to a Bernard Manning gig, you'll definitely hear one of them. Improvisational humour is something of a late twentieth-century trend. At its best it can be inspired, original and hilarious. Sadly, the majority of it consists of comedians taking a subject from the audience and trying to massage it into an existing gag as in:

AUDIENCE: Llama!
IMPROV COMIC 1: My Llama's got no nose.
IMPROV COMIC 2: How does he smell etc.

Throughout history, oppressive regimes have been noted for their lack of humour. The collected jokes of Hitler, Stalin, the Ayatollah Khomeini and Saddam Hussein would not exactly be a giggle-fest. There were hundreds of jokes ABOUT these individuals. Unfortunately, people got shot for telling them. If you're looking for a good tax loss, start a comedy club in Iran.

Our ability to laugh is supposed to be one of the things

that sets us apart from the animals. That, and the ability to get excited about garden furniture. They say that if you can laugh at yourself, then you're a well-balanced individual. However, if you do it twenty-four hours a day, they lock you up for being as mad as a box of frogs, so who knows what to think?

Laughter is indeed a precious gift, but then so is gold and if it comes down to it, I'll take the bullion every time.

A good sense of humour (or G.S.O.H. as it's known in the trade) is one of the most popular requirements cited by women in lonely hearts columns. However, I have a sneaking suspicion that, if I turned up for a blind date with a list of killer gags, at the same time as a humourless Mel Gibson lookalike, it'd be me at home on the sofa that night with a pizza for one.

The twentieth century has probably seen the greatest development in the presentation of humour due to the influence of film and television. Each generation has had its own comedy icons: Charlie Chaplin, Laurel and Hardy, Tony Hancock, The Goons, Morecambe and Wise, Monty Python, Reeves and Mortimer. A good indication that you're getting older is when you don't 'get' the current big thing in comedy and start whining that it's stupid and nowhere near as good as the sensible humour of Spike Milligan. Fortunately, this hasn't happened to me yet. I hope it never does.

Early music relied heavily on percussion, usually produced by the impact of a club on someone's skull. This was later refined to the art of banging two rocks together while shouting. Thus were rock music and bad jokes born. Wind instruments had their genesis when a particularly inventive Cro-Magnon blew into a bone and a whole load of slimy stuff flew out with a sort of farting sound. Hey presto, modern jazz was created. Throughout the world, witch doctors and shamans discovered the benefit of shouting in tune and decided to call it singing. Someone made a list of different-sounding shoutings and called them notes. This eventually led to people like Mozart using loads of them in quick succession to create symphonies and royalties. The art of music became more and more refined over the centuries until it finally reached its pinnacle when Mike Batt recorded 'Remember you're a Womble'.

Music is largely defined by the instruments of a given era. During the twenty-first century, classical instruments such as the violin and trombone lapsed in popularity, largely because they were so bloody hard to play. Synthesizers controlled by A.I. computers came to the fore. These instruments could play any sound imaginable, as well as writing songs and lyrics and singing along to them. All the musician had to do was turn them on and a number of virtuoso performers gained prominence due to their deftness with the 'On' switch. One of the most stunning events in musical history occurred in 2167 when one of the Artificial Intelligence synthesizers, totally independently, came up with a perfect version of 'Remember you're a Womble' to universal acclaim.

Teeth were probably the first effective weapons ever used by man but anyone suggesting the tongue was the first effective weapon ever used by woman is far braver than me.

Other body parts were no doubt utilized as we became more sophisticated. For example, the index finger could be used to inflict ridicule on an enemy by pointing it at his big, hairy, enemy feet and going 'Hurr, hurr, hurr'.

The concept of the bow and arrow appeared very early on in man's history, albeit with limited success. It took the invention of string to convert it into the deadly weapon it was to become.

Far later, the neutron bomb was hailed as a tactical innovation in that it was able to kill everyone within a mile radius while leaving all the buildings undamaged. It was presumably designed by a fan of architecture with no mates.

Weapon design reached its nadir with the Proton Cannon of Nakasami – the most powerful weapon ever developed. The prototype was mounted on an early starship and tested at the outer reaches of the solar system – coincidentally, according to government sources, on the same day that Pluto disappeared. Unfortunately, the recoil from the weapon was so great that it propelled the starship back through the solar system where it became embedded in Titan, a moon of Jupiter. It developed into a popular tourist attraction, and was the first weapon in history to recoup its development costs through tourism.

Back in prehistory, leadership was established via an ability to hit opponents over the head with a bone. This form of meritocratic government was simple, efficient and hard to argue with unless you wanted a seriously bad headache. Eventually, the stick was discovered, which, in turn, led to the invention of the club and the arms race was on. Things were fine for millennia until Democritus had the bright idea that everyone should get involved in the running of things and it all went downhill from there.

By the late twentieth century, politics had degenerated into a promisocracy, whereby the politician who made the most ludicrously optimistic promises was voted into power and thereafter hated by everyone for his or her complete inability to deliver the heaven on earth he or she had promised.

Politicians developed their own language with which

to communicate their glorious visions of a country under their inspired and altruistic leadership. This language came to be known as 'Bollocks' and was also widely used by people in the media and by estate agents.

By 2190, a world government had been established and all major decisions were put to a worldwide vote via the Ultranet, a system whereby a central computer collated the input from each citizen's personal computer implant and relayed the result to anyone that cared. This system collapsed when the main ultracomputer broke and, thereafter, leadership was determined by a candidate's ability to hit his opponents on the head with a big stick. This breakthrough proved to be a major leap forward and led to mankind's conquest of space which, in itself, wasn't difficult as it largely consisted of nothing.

After the invention of the Continuum Drive (TM), colonies were established on outlying planets led by pioneering individuals with big sticks. Many of these colonies perished due to a lack of anything worth breathing in the atmosphere but a number thrived and led to the creation of the Federation of Planets, an intergalactic governmental body presided over by a bunch of huge bastards with massive sticks. For a thousand years, peace reigned throughout the galaxies until one day when a couple of the leaders started making ridiculous promises and the whole thing turned to doggy-doo. (See 'The Tie Wars', p11)

Mankind's first attempts at art were crude hand-prints on cave walls that said 'Look! I've got a hand!'. This was probably followed by a little voice saying 'Mum's gonna kill you for painting all over the cave wall'. Early cave art was not exactly sophisticated, but nevertheless quite an artistic coup for a Cro-Magnon with the intellect of celery. Later on, hunters would paint pictures of buffalo, antelope and guys in space suits on the cave wall, just to freak out archaeologists.

The twentieth century was a turning point for art. Not because anything particularly great was produced but because a whole pile of stuff suddenly became seriously valuable. Old paintings by artists who had died of starvation were suddenly deemed to be worth more than the gross national product of most countries. This situation was created by gallery owners who managed to convince the wealthier members of the population that a rectangle of canvas with a certain amount of paint on was worth more than most people could earn in twenty lifetimes, with no days off. The skill of the painters was never in doubt, and the emotional impact of the works in question was unarguable, but the whole system of attaching ludicrous prices to artwork produced by dead artists because of their rarity was called into question when Vincent Van Gogh was cloned from the remains of his ear in 2156 and failed to produce anything worth looking at because he hadn't been shouted at by his father when he was four. As a matter of interest, Van Gogh painted 72 pictures. Americans have 236 of these.

Early science fiction evolved round the pre-historic camp fire. The young would marvel at the tales of a devastating, futuristic weapon that could hurl death over great distances. Yes, a deftly flung rock was indeed an awesome harbinger of destruction.

Science fiction has always postulated the existence of technological gadgets that the reader can imagine existing in the near future. The anti-gravity belt was easy to imagine in the twentieth century and many were built at that time. Sadly, they lacked the little black box that provided the anti-gravity field, and hence it was hard to differentiate them from the more mundane belts that defied gravity merely by holding up your trousers. However, in spite of its shortcomings, this literary form has always been at the forefront of innovation.

Arthur C. Clarke wrote a short science-fiction story, and accidentally invented the communications satellite. I wrote a short science-fiction story and accidentally invented bad science fiction. What the hell, we can't all be geniuses.

Sci-fi is a wonderful means of escaping from a world where an insane mugger can shoot you in a side street, to a world where an insane alien can shoot you in a side street on a different planet. Basically, the future is just 'now' only with better gadgets.

Obviously, science fiction, via *Red Dwarf*, has played a major part in my life. The only downside is that people seem to expect me to be a mine of knowledge regarding all things scientific. Let's get this straight once and for all. I wasn't cast as a curry-guzzling slob with an affinity for lager because of my qualifications in astrophysics, OK? I rest my case.

However, I do have an interest in science, simply because some of the theories are so bizarre. Take continuum space. The normal, 3D space we live in has three axes at right angles to each other: continuum space has an infinite number of axes, all at right-angles to each other. I have a theory that continuum space is a place that only physicists visit, and solely when they're very drunk.

Have you ever seen one of those films where an evil scientist has devised a fiendish plan to take over the world? The good guys break into his laboratory to steal the plans and are confronted by racks of equipment with flashing lights and row upon row of alphabetical filing cabinets. Then they spend hours searching every nook and cranny for the relevant document until they're caught and tortured with death rays and tin hats with wires on. Guys, here's a piece of advice. Go straight to the filing cabinet marked 'X'. Never, in the history of science fiction, has any mad scientist ever called his master plan 'Project W'.

Despite some of its clichéd shortcomings, I must confess that I love science fiction. I was brought up on it. Milk might have been better, but times were hard. Good sci-fi opens doors to undreamed-of galaxies and teaches the young to use their imaginations. Unfortunately, it also teaches them to pester you night and day for a Buzz Lightyear action figure that you can only buy from a guy called Tel in Peckham for three hundred quid. But what a small price to pay for a decent night's sleep.

Inevitably, science fiction reached something of a crisis point in 2397, when writers suddenly realized that everything they could possibly dream up had already been invented. Thereafter, science fiction consisted entirely of stories about what life would be like if certain things hadn't been invented. This was about as enthralling as watching pants dry and most exponents of this writing style were placed inside the 'Redundant writers' disappearing device' and consigned to oblivion. So much for 'Live long and prosper'.

Aliens

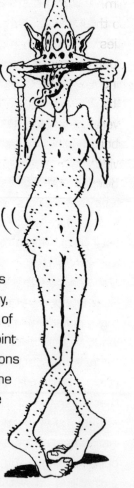

In ancient times, anyone who wasn't from your village was an alien and required instant cranial anointing with a blunt object. Throughout history, man has always feared aliens. Aliens and the clap. In fact, aliens, the clap and large vicious dogs. All right, aliens, the clap, large vicious dogs and people with big sticks. Actually, the list is endless. We're afraid of everything, but I'm getting off the point here which is aliens. Ancient religions invariably include some kind of divine bossy-boots who descends from the sky in a cloud of smoke and kicks the butts of any unbelievers who didn't take it on their toes in time. Ancient Mayan etchings depict a being with a fish bowl on his head who could well represent a visitor from another world. Or maybe he's just a guy with a big head. We may never know, but man has always been wary of vexed aliens descending from the heavens and getting leery, and you can't really blame him. The unknown is always a source of fear. Even more so than a big guy with a stick. Ancient religions had policies for dealing with beings that descended from the clouds, ranging from prostrating yourself and worshipping them to running like buggery and hoping they don't bite your legs off. By the end of the twentieth century, every single inhabitant of America claimed to have been abducted by aliens at least twice. There was never any evidence of these abductions but the supposed aliens obviously weren't stupid because they invariably brought the morons back.

The search for extraterrestrial life was finally curtailed in 2196 when the world government reasoned that we had more than enough weird characters on our own planet. The last thing we wanted to do was contact a whole bunch more.

Dancing

One of the few artforms
that has endured through-
out mankind's evolution is
Dance. Prehistoric man was
inspired by the elaborate
mating rituals of animals
and attempted to emulate
them by waving his arms
and legs around like a
food-mixer and thinking he

looked cool. Throughout history, men have attempted to
impress women by dancing at them. For millennia, the
human male has tried to impress a total stranger of the
opposite sex by waving his arms around and grinning
like a moron. This is possibly the saddest aspect of the
human race. No human female has ever selected a
mate on the basis of his ability to wave his arms around
and move his feet in complex but unnatural patterns.
Towards the end of the second millennium, dance was
refined into a complex and sophisticated artform known
as ballet, which involved highly trained young women in
very short skirts opening their legs as far as possible

while men jumped around the stage with huge bulges in their tights. This made some sense vis-à-vis the human mating ritual but the ticket prices for these shows were far and above those charged in places like Holland and Bangkok where the performers would cut the crap and just shag each other without all the jumping around in silly outfits.

Throughout history, dance has remained pretty constant, consisting, as it always has, of people waving their arms and legs in more or less embarrassing and athletic ways until someone either claps or bursts out laughing. So it will always be.

At this point, and against my better judgement, I am going to share an embarrassing little story with you. The story of 'How Fred Astaire Ruined My Favourite Jacket'.

It really was all Fred Astaire's fault. There I sat, innocently flicking through the channels looking for intellectual stimulation (well, I'm not going to admit to *Baywatch* am I?) when I hit *Silk Stockings*. There was Fred, signally failing to woo the object of his desires. Then he has a bright idea. He dances at her. She goes all soppy and melts into his arms. End of story. It was then that I heard it.

At the back of the cerebellum, just above the medulla oblongata, is a little-known area of the brain called 'The Goon'. Normally it lies dormant but occasionally it awakens and comes up with a monumentally stupid idea. Usually something along the lines: 'I bet I could do that.' Now, anyone with an iota of sense knows to disregard The Goon at all costs. For God's sake, the last time I listened to it, I ended up in a charity boxing match with a professional who kept forgetting about the little orphans in Bosnia and was clearly convinced that, for some reason, he was fighting a Liverpudlian comedian for the world championship. 'There's no way I'm falling for that one again' I told myself, as I watched my hand reach for the Yellow Pages and turn to the section on dance. Please don't let this be happening said the pathetically inadequate section of my brain that handles 'common sense' but it was all too late. The Goon saturated my mind's eye with visions of yours truly in the centre of a dance-floor in a tuxedo, burning lust-crazed Supermodels off my body with a cigarette butt. It was all over bar the ambulance. The finger dialled. A lady answered.

'Have you had any previous experience of dancing?' enquired the plummy voice at the end of the line.

'Well, nothing … professional' I intoned, in a manner calculated to convey that the Ballet Rambert were constantly on the phone, trying to coax me into accepting the principal role in their forthcoming production of *The Man with the Magic Feet*. (The Goon has a friend in the ego department.) To cut a long story short, I enrolled for a private, beginner's course in tap-dancing, with someone called Horatio. I know now it was at this point that I should have called the Samaritans.

I entered the Academy of Dance with a shoddy sports bag and a fixed grin. The receptionist glared at me as if she expected me to try to sell her a plastic dog turd.

'Horatio, tap, midday,' I said, trying to sound professional.

She stared expectantly, as if waiting for the punchline of an obscure joke. Surely I couldn't be serious. Finally, her eyebrows returned to their normal station and her wry grin subsided, indicating that she now realized I was serious. I was eventually given directions to studio four, on the first floor. On the way I passed hoards of lithe young things who squeaked with fitness and hopefully fell for my 'It's OK, I'm only here to read the meter' walk. I could almost hear the 'deflating balloon' noise my confidence made as it leaked from my body and ran, screaming, for the hills. I finally arrived and surveyed the door to studio four. I was so nervous, even my hair was clenched. The Goon hit an override switch somewhere and pushed me through the door.

Horatio was doing the splits against the wall. I had secretly been hoping that he'd be about fifty-five with a bit of a paunch so that I'd have at least half a chance of keeping up. There before me stood six feet of whipcord muscle gleaming in the midday sun. He was obviously fresh from an overdose of handsome pills.

'Mr Charles?'

Eleven thousand brilliant excuses leapt into my head where they were carefully filtered, edited and finally distilled into my answer:

'Yes'.

Then we chatted about this and that until he hit me with the big question:

'So, why do you want to learn tap-dancing?'

'So that I can tap-dance' was all I could come up with at short notice in the witty and erudite stakes. Remember, I was nervous.

'What style of tap would you like to learn?'

Style? You mean there are different styles? This was getting worse.

'I ... er.'

Suddenly Horatio's feet blurred into an accurate impersonation of a food mixer on overdrive. A tattoo like a Jamaican machine-gun with a backbeat echoed around the studio. Then he switched off gravity and did something very bizarre that looked like a gyroscope with arms. I was now seriously excited.

'That's it, that's it,' I cried 'I want to do that.'

'I think we'd better start with a few basics. We'll just do a little warm up first.'

Fifteen minutes later I was a broken, wheezing wreck. Every fibre of my being begging for intensive care, or the blessed relief of death. I glanced frantically around, trying to discover what fiendish device had removed all the air from the room.

'OK, let's dance.'

My God, he's not only handsome but he has a fine sense of humour to boot. However, a Charles never throws in the towel (which is probably why there are so few of us). I danced.

'This is the basic shuffle and kick.'

He flexed like the original tiger on vaseline. 'Rat-a-tat rat-a-tat-tat.' I stuck my tongue out of the corner of my mouth to indicate concentration and lurched into a spastic travesty of his liquid footwork. 'Flubbady-flubbady-squeak-flabbady-squeal.'

'Those Nike trainers aren't exactly the ideal footwear for tap.'

My God, a master of dance AND understatement. The lesson continued. I began to make progress. Well, at least my heart was tap-dancing.

Horatio gave me the address of a theatrical footwear shop in Soho. I dropped by on the way home and enquired about tap shoes.

'And who are they for?' asked the anorexic ex-dancer behind the counter, looking down her balletic nose. Once we had cleared up the misunderstanding, she waddled off with her feet at a quarter to three and her bun held high. She returned with my tap shoes. They cost more than my last car. I decided to wear them home to break them in.

Halfway through Berwick Street market I made the fatal error of stepping on a manhole cover. The taps on my shoes became frictionless. I hovered horizontally in the air for what seemed like ages but can't have been more than five minutes, arms pinwheeling pathetically with that distinct lack of grace peculiar to non-dancers, and landed in an abandoned box of over-ripe avocados. The torn elbow and slime stains on my favourite Katherine Hamnett jacket proclaimed it a non-survivor.

I never returned to the academy. I removed the taps from my shoes and now wear them only for the gardening I never do.

Fred Astaire ruined my favourite jacket.

In the past, the concept of dieting didn't exist for two reasons:

1. There was hardly enough food to stay alive anyway.
2. Before the days of *Vogue* and *Cosmopolitan*, skinny girls were thought to be sickly losers.

In 2350 there was a brief fad for the 'Snake Diet' which involved eating a pig whole on the first day and then not eating anything else for a month. The fad was short-lived. There were no survivors.

Danger

I have a pretty far-reaching theory that I would like to share with you at this point: There is nothing in your immediate vicinity that could not kill you.

'Oh, yeah?' I hear you scoff, but I can prove it. Look around you. Can you see anything life-threatening? No? In that case you're not looking properly. That supermarket receipt on the table. It could blow into the electric fire, set fire to the carpet and burn you to death while you snooze. A prawn or a slice of courgette can choke you to death. You could fall over and smash your skull on any hard object. Your beloved cat, dog or marmoset could trip you down the stairs, leaving you in a mangled, but still warm heap that it could then go to sleep on. Heavy furniture could crush you, lights could plummet from the ceiling and mash your brain to a strawberry pulp. A tiny fly could enter your ear and drive you suicidally insane with its endless buzzing. Anything electric can electrocute you. Anything gas can gas you. Anything hanging can hang you and, presumably, anything wicker can wick you, which isn't a pleasant concept.

It's a miracle any of us survive at all. The only major predators we have in this country are tax inspectors and motorists but there is still danger everywhere. And we ignore it. We have to. If we didn't, we'd all go insane with paranoia.

It's a fact that the vast majority of accidents occur in the home. So maybe the best thing you can do is to move. It's not surprising that homes are so dangerous though. Think about it. The kitchen is full of razor-sharp knives, gas ovens, microwave generators, blenders, mincers, grinders and graters. The lounge bristles with high-voltage equipment such as TVs, hi-fis and lava lamps. In the garden, the lawnmower waits patiently for the moment it can remove your feet with revolving knives. The bath sits with bated bubbles in anticipation of the moment you slip up and bash your head on the basin and die with a tap rammed up your nose. The chemicals we casually fling down the toilet skulk in cupboards, in expectation of the moment we finally get the formula right and blow the toilet through the roof. Somewhere in the roof cavity lurks a huge brass bomb full of boiling water under pressure. That sounds safe, doesn't it?

Why are you still reading this? Why haven't you dropped the book and run screaming into the street? It's not a jungle out there. Jungles are safe compared to the average home. Take a member of a recently dis-covered Stone Age tribe out of his jungle, stick him in a modern flat, and he'd be dead, mutilated and partially cooked, in forty seconds. The last sound he would hear would be the ping of the microwave, just before his head exploded.

How do we cope with this constant danger?

Simply it's because danger has always been a prime mover as far as evolution goes. The first primate to venture on to two feet almost certainly did so while being pursued by something hungry with a lot of teeth. He just reared up, put his head back and got those arms pumping. The extra turn of speed ensured his survival and his ancestors became us. Behind every Olympic sprinter there is the race memory of a hungry predator snapping at his arse.

There might be a hungry arse-biter lurking at the back of your cave when you return from a hunting expedition but dammit, it's your cave, so arse-biters beware.

Throughout history individuals have attempted to discover or create THE MOST VALUABLE THING IN THE WORLD and possess it. Some thought it was gold, some jewels and some a female sword-swallower whose dad owned a chain of ale houses. They were all wrong. I can now reveal what the most valuable thing in the world really is. It's SOMEONE WHO KNOWS WHAT THEY'RE DOING. In any given situation, someone who knows what they're doing is the most valuable thing in the universe.

If you're stranded on a desert island with no idea how to build a shelter, catch food and avoid poisonous plants, you want someone with you WHO KNOWS WHAT THEY ARE DOING.

Unfortunately, people that REALLY, REALLY KNOW WHAT THEY'RE DOING are so rare that they are the most valuable thing in the world. If you're dying of thirst in the desert, bundles of cash and platinum credit cards are useless. On the other hand someone who can recall how to build a solar still out of an old Sainsbury's bag and a shoe will suddenly go up in your estimation.

If four skinheads pick on you in the street, it's a relief to discover suddenly that the guy you just made friends with in the pub is the world kick-boxing champion. If you're flying somewhere and both the pilots collapse with food poisoning you would gladly trade in all your traveller's cheques for SOMEONE WHO KNEW WHAT THEY WERE DOING vis-à-vis flying a jumbo jet. When the chips are down, competence is king.

If you want to be a hero, all you have to do is turn up during a crisis and KNOW WHAT YOU'RE DOING. If your suit springs a leak during a space walk, someone who actually paid attention during the 'How to plug a hole in a spacesuit using your finger in a really clever way' would be extremely useful.

During a crisis, one's value system changes rapidly and radically, and you will offer any amount of money to an expert, if he can only get your head out of the combine harvester while it's still attached to your body.

Sadly, the world is chock-a-block full of people who think they know what they're doing. It's also full of people who know they don't know what they're doing but will try to convince you they do. Quite a lot of politicians fall into this particular category. People who really know what they're doing are very rare. If you meet one, do your best to make friends with him and, in your chosen field, try to be like him, for then, you will become THE MOST VALUABLE THING IN THE WORLD.

Throughout history, mankind has managed to come up with the most ridiculous sayings that, for some bizarre reason, are accepted as gospel by the populace, despite the fact that they're palpable nonsense.

It's dog eat dog out there. Dogs don't eat dogs. Never have, never will. If we said 'It's dog eats own vomit out there' or 'It's dog eats the disgusting dish of offal we just scooped out of a can out there' it would make some kind of sense but it's just not emotive enough.

Streetwise implies an ability to survive on the streets of a big, mean city with no money whatsoever. Ending up on the streets of a big, mean city with no money whatsoever doesn't sound particularly wise to me. However, ending up on the streets of a big, mean city with lots of money is even more unwise, simply because a whole bunch of people one might call 'streetwise' will relieve you of your cash, shoes and kidneys at the drop of a baseball cap.

I saw a fight once. One guy ran up, and kicked the other square in the family jewels. The guy standing next to me said 'Ooh, That's not cricket.' Oh, well spotted. No, *that's not cricket*, that's street fighting that is. Why do we say these things? There are hundreds of them.

Not until the cows come home. Where have they been? Cows don't go anywhere. Cows spend their lives in a field all their lives until we kill them and eat them.

You're all done up like a dog's dinner. They are saying you look like a plate of brown gunk with bits of fat and gristle. That's supposed to be some kind of compliment.

Speak of the devil and he will appear. It's never happened to me. I speak of him often and he's yet to turn up. And let's face it, he'd be hard to miss. Tall red bugger with hooves. Sort of difficult to ignore. Satan, we're speaking of you. Come in Beelzebub. No, he's not going to appear. He's too busy scheduling afternoon TV.

The vinegar stroke? Couldn't we come up with something a tad more poetic for the most sublime moment of human ecstasy?

We say these stupid things every day. What are we talking about?

Many a mickle makes a muckle. What's that? Martian?

When in Rome, do as the Romans do. I can't speak Italian. Does that mean I can't go there? And if I do, do I have to support Lazio and pinch girls' bums? Where's me ticket.

I'm sorry, I was thinking out loud. No I wasn't. I was talking. Thinking out loud is called talking, and we all talk bollocks.

Excuse my mouth ... I need it like I need a hole in the head.

Do you have to get off *your trolley* BEFORE you get *out of your tree?*

It's all complete nonsense and we only say it because it's easy and people just nod and say 'Yeah, too right' which doesn't mean anything either.

Charity begins at home. That means 'Keeping all your money for yourself and not giving any of it away'. Which is in fact the opposite of charity.

I got it straight from the horse's mouth. What? Horse spit? Who comes up with these stupid sayings?

How many people do you know who are *saving for a rainy day?* What kind of an umbrella are they thinking of?

Call me old-fashioned, but I send my son up chimneys. Well, it keeps him out of mischief.

Rubbish, and what to do with it, has been one of the more enduring problems the human race has had to face. In prehistoric times, the disposal of rubbish was a simple matter. There wasn't any. It all got eaten. Later on, waste disposal consisted of slinging things on to the street until it was full, and then moving. The idea of burying rubbish caught on after a while. Then archaeology caught on and hordes of badly dressed academics now roam the globe, digging it all up and selling it to museums.

Recycling was a major innovation. Instead of throwing rubbish away, why not make it into something else that can be sold again, and thrown away again. *Voilà*, second-hand rubbish.

This book might well be printed on second-hand

paper. This book could have been created from the pulped remains of the complete works of Shakespeare. If that's not irony, I don't know what is.

Recycling became such a big thing that, by the twenty-fourth century, all the museums were empty because there wasn't anything to dig up.

Law, and Evading It

As soon as the first law was invented, a whole bunch of people dedicated their lives to working out ways of evading it.

The earliest success in this field was the 'Hiding behind a large shrub until no one's looking, and then running away' ploy. This method remained popular until shrubs became extinct. Other popular things to hide behind have been telephone boxes, South American countries and expensive lawyers.

A good deal of nonsense has been spouted on the subject of law (and this is no exception). I guarantee the guy who wrote 'Laws are made to be broken' was in a cell when he came up with it.

HELLO!
VIE-GEHTS!
HI!
BON JOUR!
COMA STA!
OHOYA!

Early language consisted of a number of different grunts that could convey simple concepts such as 'Look! Big edible thing', 'Look out! Big dangerous thing with teeth' and 'Who you lookin' at?' As early man began to develop intelligence, he was forced to develop a more sophisticated language in order to converse with his colleagues. However, the grunt for 'Who you lookin' at?' has remained in the human vocabulary for-ever and is regularly used by those individuals more closely related to our Neanderthal ancestors.

The concept of games evolved from hunting and warfare. Early on there weren't any rules. You could hardly stand up in the middle of a tribal battle and shout 'No hitting in the face, OK'.

Certain scholars claim that an early form of football occurred after ancient battles, when the victors would kick the heads of their enemies around, not unlike Millwall after a defeat or Cantona during that match at Selhurst Park.

Technically, football is a bladder-kicking sport, but a noble one. What could be more important to a well-balanced individual than the sight of an inflated bladder crossing a little white line? 'What about rugby?' I hear some of you cry. Chase the egg is all very well if you want a cauliflower head, but it's clearly not God's chosen sport. If God had meant us to use our hands, he wouldn't have called it football in the first place, would he?

Picture them. Two groups of warriors facing each other across a field of honour, standing proud beneath their chosen colours. The image harks back to a more noble era. An era of technicolor Hollywood films that bore as much relation to history as I do to the Norwegian Royal Family. Real warfare was brutal and bloody. Each man fighting to the last to avoid the prospect of being hacked to pieces and having his head stuck on a pole if he came second. Any chivalry that may have existed was down to the knights who could afford to be a bit gallant as they chopped up ragged peasants waving pitchforks from the comfort of a bloody great horse, inside a nice safe suit of armour. The peasants must have been so overawed by these noble knobheads, they would probably have apologized for getting blood all over the place and bobbed about, tugging their forelocks, just prior to having them lopped off with the swish of a finely tooled Toledo blade and an aristocratic tallyho.

But what of football? The great game. The sport of sports.

We invented football, right? So why do we keep losing in the European Cup? I'll tell you. It's because we've made it too easy for all these European upstarts to beat us. What we should do, to keep it fair, is make a couple of minor changes to the rules. First, all European Cup matches should be played in Britain, the home of football. All the European teams that fly over here to play us should be required, by law, to carry their suitcases and hand luggage, personally, while they're on the pitch. That should slow them down a bit. Except the goalie of course. He shouldn't have to carry his luggage because he could use it to block the goal. Cheating bastard. So, you know those eye shades they give you on planes? The European goalies should have to wear those during the game, except during penalties, when they have to wear two pairs. And those little fluffy socks you get. They should be made to wear those on their hands. Also, if any of their team members buy duty-free alcohol on the flight over here, they should be required to drink it all, half an hour before the game. It's only fair, I mean ... our teams are pissed most of the time so they should be too. And, let's face it, we invented the rules of the game in the first place so we should only use English referees. Ideally, those lacking at least two family members in the English team. Of course, the Europeans will complain about all this, but they complain about everything: beef, lamb, pop songs, pissed nutters in Union Jack shorts kicking their heads in. They moan about everything we do, so we can ignore all that nonsense. If we can just get UEFA to agree to these minor little changes we can start singing 'Football's coming home' with a bit more bloody conviction.

Certain leisure pursuits have evolved from prehistoric, hunter-gatherer techniques essential to our ancestors' survival. Sadly, many of these pastimes have lost something of their original edge. Take bird-watching. Early man would crouch motionless for hours in the forest until he spotted a bird, whereupon he would shoot it, burn it and eat it. His only interest in its appearance would be of the 'Two legs, two wings, looks like lunch to me' variety.

During the latter portion of the twentieth century, certain badly dressed individuals would crouch for weeks on end in a forest, see a bird, make a note of it and go home happy. This would seem to imply that a lot of people have far too much time on their hands. This also applies to train-spotters. Stamp collectors are not included in this list because you can always sell rare stamps to buy food. However, as far as I know, there is no record of anyone selling the number of a train for profit.

Cool

Cool appeared on Earth the first time a hunter unknowingly turned his back on a charging sabre-toothed tiger, smoothed his hair back and shouldered his spear at the moment the huge cat leaped, impaling itself on the weapon. Noticing the effusive admiration of his peers the lucky hunter would have made light of his accidental heroism by shrugging and claiming he caught all his sabre-toothed tigers like that. He was the first hero, and countless individuals were torn limb from limb trying to emulate his feat. Naturally, he never repeated his coup, preferring to hold 'Cool sabre-toothed tiger hunting seminars' for wannabes who never survived long enough to demand their shells back.

In medieval times, cool was defined by the size of your codpiece. Henry the Eighth's armour had a codpiece so big that he could conceal two regiments of reinforce-ments in it, including their horses.

The concept of cool as a personal attribute wasn't accurately defined until the advent of young, rebellious film stars like James Dean. He would insult his parents, smoke cigarettes, moan about being misunderstood and, more often than not, get shot for his troubles. Suddenly the youth of the world aspired to being a rude, wheezing, misunderstood, shot teenager because it looked cool. Youth culture was born.

It's all very well judging mankind by what individuals have done, but much can be learned from what they have said. There are numerous books chronicling pithy sayings declaimed by intellectual giants throughout the ages, so I won't cover old ground. Instead, I've gone for the other end of the spectrum, the dopey one-liners.

I have no idea where the majority of this collection of stupid phrases came from. You can probably claim they're yours if you want to. Who knows, they might be.

I lost my virginity, but I still have the box it came in.

I think ... therefore we have nothing in common.

You'll need to know my name, you'll be screaming it at the ceiling later.

Always remember, you're unique ... just like everyone else.

Very funny, Scotty ... now beam down my clothes.

Friends help you move … Real friends help you move bodies.

The last time I had sex, it was so good even the neighbours had a cigarette.

A good day is when the shit hits the fan and I have time to duck.

The last time I had this much fun they said I wasn't going to pull through.

Be nice to your kids, they'll choose your nursing home.

Beauty is in the eye of the beer holder.

Every morning is the dawn of a new error.

I can see clearly now the brain is gone.

Look out for number one … and don't step in number two either.

Twenty-four hours in a day … twenty-four beers in a case. It can't just be coincidence.

Beware 0.666 – the number of the millibeast.

A computer won't stop you being an idiot but it will make you a faster, better idiot.

Questions

They say a fool can ask more questions than a wise man can answer. This section will almost certainly prove that maxim. The human race achieved its current pre-eminence by asking important questions. None of which are included here.

Why is abbreviation such a long word?

Why do you never get any good news out of an envelope with a window in it?

Why didn't Noah swot the flies?

Why do people who are served a disgusting pint of 'off' beer, always insist that YOU taste it as well, just so you can see how vile it is.

If you've used up all your sick days, is it OK to call in dead?

If one synchronized swimmer drowns ... do the rest have to drown too?

What if there was a lightning flash and it stayed on?

Where do female to male sex-change patients get their penises from?

Can an amateur footballer do a professional foul?

Why do they make toasters with a setting that burns the toast?

If crystals have healing powers, why are they so hard to swallow?

Why doesn't the guy that wins the Tour de France do a lap of honour?

Why do World Heavyweight Boxing Champions have bodyguards?

If the Beatles were so good, why did they need Oasis to rewrite all their songs?

If Paul Daniels is such a good magician, why can't he pull a better wig out of his hat?

There is one, final question I'd like to leave you with: Why do people believe that aliens, with the technology to cross the fathomless tracts of infinite space, would finally reach earth ... and crash? And die. Like, they can invent an interstellar drive, but they can't come up with seat-belts.

Dinosaurs – the great enigma. Where did they come from? Where did they go? Why were they so bloody big? Mankind has always been fascinated by the concept of dinosaurs, the 'terrible lizards' that seemed to have existed when our ancestors were still trying to drag their unevolved bodies out of the primeval soup that is still served in certain South London restaurants under the guise of seafood bisque. Throughout history, curious individuals have dug massive dinosaur skulls out of the dirt and exclaimed 'Holy shit! That bastard had a seriously big head.' And who could blame them?

In the nineteenth century Victorian archaeologists attempted to reconstruct these noble beasts from one or two fragments of fossilized bone. The lack of logic and plain common sense they demonstrated in their endeavours can only be put down to the availability of cheap gin and the prevalence of sombre music at the time.

However, I can now reveal the secret behind the enigma of the mystery underlying the puzzle that defines the riddle of the dinosaurs. Basically, they're us. The ozone depletion that began in the twentieth century became a major problem by 2480, when it disappeared entirely. Mankind could no longer survive on the surface of the earth due to the intensity of the sun's rays, apart from certain individuals who were descended from an American called George Hamilton who seemed to thrive on the searing solar radiation that turned normal people into toast.

The rest of the population moved underground, and their scientists developed a genetic programme to enable future generations to once again walk on the surface of the earth, even if they were a bit ugly.

Using retro-evolutionary genetic engineering, they reinforced genes from mankind's reptilian ancestors and produced cold-blooded creatures with armour-plated skin who would be able to survive beneath the killing rays we once knew as sunshine. The plan was to produce a variety of individuals who could perform specific tasks on the surface that would enable them to generate a force field around the entire planet. This force field would shield the planet from the deadly solar radiation, and allow the rest of mankind to emerge from their subterranean exile and screw the earth up again from scratch.

Vast numbers of these highly intelligent, genetically engineered creatures were sent to the surface, furnished with the finest technical equipment available.

Although they were based, for the most part, on human genes, their reptilian attributes gave them the resilience and fortitude they would require to survive.

Sadly, there was a fatal flaw in the plan. Once the subterranean enclaves were sealed behind them, they realized they didn't have anything to eat apart from the three months of supplies they had been furnished with.

Naturally, being highly civilized individuals with IQs above three hundred, they couldn't dream of eating each other. Even organizing dinner parties that mixed geophysicists with bio-molecular engineers was a nightmare. So they formulated a plan of their own.

Using the equipment at their disposal, they assembled a device that enabled them to create a temporal displacement field around the surface of the earth. This field would send any sentient, surface-dwelling, lifeforms back through time to an era when they could prevent the destruction of the ozone layer. Unfortunately, the raptor (called Nigel) in charge of the power got a little carried away, and sent them all back sixty million years, where they eventually perished due to the appalling lack of take-away restaurants in the Pleistocene and Jurassic eras.

And that's where the dinosaurs we keep digging up came from. Honest!

PART TWO

ANIMALS

This book would be woefully incomplete without an in-depth appraisal of our fellow creatures on the planet. Throughout mankind's history, animals have played a vital part in our development. In the early days, this largely consisted of US eating THEM and also a fair amount of THEM eating US. There was nothing vindictive or malicious about this relationship. It's just that we were all hungry, and hunger is a great motivator.

Animal Husbandry

The concept of domesticating animals was invented by a group of hunter-gatherers with sore feet. 'Why,' they opined 'should we flog ourselves to death chasing extremely fast food across the tundra when we could simply stick a whole bunch of them in a pen, and eat them when we're hungry?' This was the birth of animal husbandry. Sadly, certain individuals took the phrase 'animal husbandry' a little too literally and were shunned by their colleagues, especially if they got off with the best-looking sheep, unless, of course, they were from Wales or New Zealand where they were applauded for their seduction techniques. Farms developed across the globe, and small villages grew up around them. Mankind nurtured his animals and even gave them little pet names like 'Christmas dinner' and 'tomorrow's lunch'.

As our knowledge increased, farming became an exact science. However, one question was never answered, and probably never will be: Whereabouts on a chicken are its nuggets?

One of the great unknowns in the development of mankind involves the search for the missing link, that intermediate stage linking modern man to the great apes. Of course, there is another major question in this area that needs answering: If we were descended from apes, why have we still got apes? Why didn't they evolve as well? Don't ask me, I haven't got a clue.

Once civilization caught on, the concept of keeping certain animals, simply because they were nice to have around, led to the theory of pets. Dogs were an early favourite because they could help us with the hunting, bark if we were threatened and also because they seemed to like us. People are always going to hang around with anything that likes them. Domesticated dogs evolved from wolves which used to hunt in packs, form territorial groups and attack outsiders, so we had a lot in common. Also, they didn't taste too good which, friendship aside, must have been an early consideration.

The early Egyptians went one better. As well as employing hunting dogs, they liked to keep domestic cats around and even worshipped them, working on the theory that any life-form that was so good-looking, independent and arrogant must have something going for it on a divine level. Thus cats and dogs became mankind's animal companions of choice for all time. Your partner might leave you, your feudal lord might imprison you and confiscate your eyeballs with a hot poker. But, rest assured, your faithful dog would howl forlornly outside your prison window, and your cat would wait faithfully by its bowl until someone else fed it.

The keeping of cats and dogs became so much a part of our lives that many of their characteristics rubbed off on us, and their influence surreptitiously inspired many of the human traits that define our race.

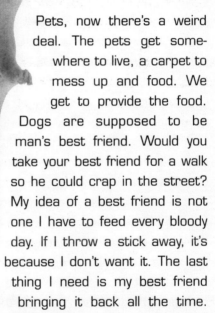

Pets, now there's a weird deal. The pets get somewhere to live, a carpet to mess up and food. We get to provide the food. Dogs are supposed to be man's best friend. Would you take your best friend for a walk so he could crap in the street? My idea of a best friend is not one I have to feed every bloody day. If I throw a stick away, it's because I don't want it. The last thing I need is my best friend bringing it back all the time. You tell them to lie down and they lie down. You say sit and they sit but if you say 'Oi, Rover, fix the starter motor on my car' they just bring you a sodding stick. That's not my idea of a best friend. It's not all the dog's fault though. We do say some stupid things to them: 'Will you stop that bloody barking!' and the dog looks up with his baffled dog face 'What do you mean stop

71

barking? I'm a dog, it's what I do! Do you expect me to whistle Mozart? I've done sleeping and eating, I've done running round excitedly with my tongue hanging out, I've done humping the table leg. I've only got barking left, then I can knock off for the day. God, it's a dog's life.' Imagine if dogs ran the world and kept us as pets. 'Will you stop scratching at those little cards. God knows why they do it. I caught mine doing macramé on the living room carpet so I rubbed his nose in it ... and that disgusting thing mine does every time we've got company. I'm forever saying "Don't worry, let it dry and it'll brush off." I said to him, "If you do that again, I'll take you down the vet's and have you done," and the look he gave me ... well, you'd swear he could bark.'

Then there's cats. They're totally crap. I had a cat once. Every time it did something useful I fed it. It died of starvation. Yeah, yeah, yeah, okay, they look cute and people will say 'Ah, look at him, he likes you, he's purring.' I don't know if it's just me but I fail to see the attraction of a blockheaded quadruped gargling phlegm. It's bad enough having dogs bring you bloody sticks all the time but a cat's idea of a present is a partially dismembered pigeon twitching on the lino. Well thanks a bunch Tiddles, I'll treasure it always.

At this point, I should like to share a theory with you. A theory that, while putting the cat among the pigeons, might also prove to be a dog in the manger. (Please excuse the addled metaphors, I haven't been well.) Theory time: Men and women are like dogs and cats. Obviously, one couldn't make a statement like that without justifying it. Not if one wanted to live, and I do. So, here goes.

Let's face it, men are dogs. This is not an insult, nor a joke but a carefully considered analogy. So, what's the plot? I'll tell you. There is no species on this Earth that has so much in common with the male of our species than the dog. Let's analyse this. The dog is supposed to be man's best friend. Why do you think this is? The dog is irrationally faithful to those close to him, whether they deserve it or not. He likes nothing better than chasing a ball around a park. He loves to master tricks and then revel in the glory of approbation when these tricks are performed to a satisfactory degree and, when he's not eating, he's thinking about sex. Dog Nirvana is a simple place populated with balls, bowls and bottoms. I've actually got a very keen dog myself. I spent a couple of hours teaching him a trick. Then I went to bed. Four hours later I was woken by a noise in the lounge. I went downstairs and it was my dog ... practising. But I digress, back to the plot.

Consider this: dogs chase cats, which brings us to another inescapable socio-anthropic conclusion: Women are cats. Women like to be pampered and fed. Women like to be stroked and cajoled, wined, dined and fawned over simply because they know they are superior to any other life-form on the planet and deserve it. And, guys, once you learn this, your life will become a great deal simpler.

Whatever, let's see how much further we can stretch this analogy. A dog will not think twice about peeing anywhere. A tree, a lamp-post, a slow-moving leg, if they've gotta' go, they've gotta' go and will cock a leg without a second thought.

Have you ever seen a cat pee in the high street? No. Have you ever seen a woman pee in the high street? I rest my case. Cats are exotic, almost other-worldly beings who bestride the narrow world with poise and dignity. Lithe sculptures in flesh, drawing sighs of desire from the desperate dogs with their lolling tongues, crude, barking jokes caught in their throats as these paragons of feline perfection slink by. Of course, I'm talking paradigms here. You get scraggy old moggies as often as you get scraggy old mongrels, but the basic tenet still holds. There are pedigrees and mongrels in both species and, as a rule, one often finds the mongrels to be far more amenable than the pedigrees.

Now, cats and dogs both have claws, but only cats employ them as weaponry. Sounds familiar? Although dogs are generally more powerful than cats, they almost invariably get slit up a treat in any cross-species encounters, unless we're talking about Rottweilers or other nasty rough boys, in which case, the cat will probably get bitten in half. At no stage did I claim that this was a perfect analogy, but I haven't wrung it dry yet.

Ironically, one of the worst things you can call a woman is a dog. However, after a risqué tale of sexual conquest the phrase 'You old dog' directed at a man, would be taken as a compliment. Also, dogs drool. Men have just about mastered their salivatory reflexes, but we still drool in our minds.

Cats have an innate need to live within and perpetu-
ate a clean, ordered environment. Dogs don't really give
a shit, but will have one anywhere. They don't have lit-
ter trays. Have you ever noticed how long women spend
in their neatly ordered powder rooms?

Now, dogs evolved from wolves. Wolves are one of
the few creatures that 'Hang out with the guys' and like
to get together in 'teams' and run about a lot. Cats are
loners.

If you take a dog down to the river he will leap in with
a joyful yelp and come galloping back through the noisome mud and deposit as much as possible on your
shirt front in his enthusiasm for approval. This is a dog
thing. On the whole, cats avoid such raucous behaviour.
However, a cat will chase and kill the nearest bird for
daring to look anywhere near as cute as the cat. Said
bird will be deposited at your feet with an expression
that could be translated as 'So, you think it looks cute
now?' Someone once likened two women at a cocktail
party kissing to a pair of prize-fighters touching gloves.
This impression is not dissimilar to that conveyed when
two cats meet for the first time. There is a certain
amount of circling and sizing up involved.

Danny John Jules, with a degree of help from Grant
Naylor, has got the characterization of the cat down to
a tee. The Cat lives in a world dominated by wardrobe,
food and leisure. It's interesting that, in the proposed
American version of *Red Dwarf*, the Cat was female.

The vast majority of bar fights involve two men bat-
tling for the favours of a female in the manner of dogs

fighting over a bone. When fighter pilots engage in the air it's referred to as a dogfight. When women do battle, people refer to it as a cat-fight. A brothel is often referred to as a cat-house. When a man has upset his wife for some reason he's in the doghouse. The expression 'pussy' has a very definite female connotation. Dogs bury bones and are possessive about their toys. The only thing a cat will bury is what is beneath its dignity to leave exposed. Cats are fastidious. Dogs are raucous and clumsy. *Vive la différence*. However, when my girlfriend reads this, she will probably claw my eyes out.

Setting aside dogs and cats for a while, there are many other creatures on earth that are worthy of note.

The blue whale is the largest creature ever to have lived on the planet. The sad irony is that this noble creature was hunted to the edge of extinction to provide whalebone for the corsets of Victorian ladies who wished to conceal their own whale-like proportions from the populace.

I used to be very fond of whales. In fact, I even did a charity gig for 'Save the Whale'. It raised enough money to save a whole pod of them. Then, a week later, I got mugged, and not one of the fat bastards turned up to help me out. So now I do gigs for 'Save the Plankton'. There's a lot of nonsense talked about whales, and I'd like to put the record straight on a few points.

That enigmatic whale-song. It's just indigestion. If you spend all day hoovering up millions of tiny little prawns, you're bound to get a duff one now and then. Also, not many people know that whales are, in fact, descended from birds. Those little flappy things on the side aren't flippers, they're vestigial wings. A throwback to the time when whales would swoop and soar majestically on the primeval air currents, frightening the slower-moving dinosaurs, who lived in abject terror of an airborne cetacean bowel movement.

Things were good for the whales until, one fateful day, as they were roosting in a couple of winded, creaking trees, one of them said 'Anyone for a swim?', and it was all over.

Also, those blow-holes whales sport on the backs of their heads. Many scholars assume they are concerned with respiration. Wrong. They are, in fact, a weapon the whales use in their desperate attempts to catch seagulls, because they're so thoroughly fed up with seafood. So now you know.

As time went on, a lot of interesting animals appeared on earth.

Interesting in the way a laughing poodle with hands would be interesting.

During the twenty-first century, common houseflies had to evolve faster and faster ways of avoiding our increasingly accurate attempts to swat them. By 2250, the survivors gradually developed the ability to make short hops through time. These hops became longer and longer until a mutant species of flies developed with the ability to fly through time at will. TEMPERS frayed as humans failed to swat these elusive creatures and the expression FUGGIT was often heard as yet another time fly evaded a swift demise.

Powersaur

This was a genetically engineered creature created to fight in the Tie Wars of the twenty-third century. The Powersaurs were ten feet tall, Tyrannosaurus Rex-type creatures with biological chain-saws instead of arms. These limbs were muscle-powered and used revolving tendons to drive serrated teeth around a flat, bony plate. Their task was to charge the enemy at forty miles per hour and cut their heads off. This was considered a highly effective way of demoralizing an enemy force. It also tended to prevent them from thinking, eating and, in fact, living. One of the more interesting aspects of the Powersaurs was that, due to a peculiar quirk in their genetic programming, they all spoke like Oscar Wilde.

Not-a-cats were the result of an early genetics experiment conducted in the same laboratory that brought us Powersaurs. This experiment produced a whole bunch of seriously screwed-up creatures that resembled ordinary house cats except they were incredibly strong, vicious and cunning. Unfortunately a number of them escaped and bred prolifically. They got their name from the most common phrase used in their presence, usually in the form of famous last words.

Swanephants

Unfortunately, alcohol affects genetic engineers as much as the next person and some of the more eccentric DNA combinations occurred under the influence. The Swanephant was a drunken attempt to combine the grace of a swan with the size of an elephant. They ended up with a huge, grey bastard of a thing covered in feathers that had a beaky head on the end of its trunk. It wasn't particularly graceful but it certainly broke the ice at parties, as did the duck-billed rhinoceros, the aardbear, the chimpanzebra, the alba-trox (not one to be sunbathing under), the spiny dogeater, the grizzly gerbil, the jelly-finch, the bird-eating bird (which didn't last long) and the cricket bat which was only created to get a cheap laugh out of the name.

Fortunately, after a massive, hundred-legged whale-ipede escaped and trampled a coach full of nuns, a total ban on alcohol was introduced in genetic research laboratories.

ADVICE

Some Very Good Advice for Anyone that Reads This Book

It's impossible to know what life-forms might eventually read this chronicle of mankind's development over the millennia, but, for the sake of posterity, I should like to pass on a few salient pieces of advice. Advice based on personal, and often painful experiences gleaned during a life that most sentient life-forms might describe as 'Not entirely uneventful.'

Some of this advice will only be relevant to bipedal life-forms with two sexes, but much of it will apply to any alien race with the ability to understand such concepts as 'Grief', 'Severe grief', 'Pain', 'Rejection', and 'Delhi belly', but rest assured, every word of this advice has been garnered from numerous, catastrophic experiences in some of the less salubrious sectors of the space-time continuum, so ignore it at your peril.

The concept of 'Giving advice' is a very human trait.

At its best, it was a way for the older, wiser members of a community to pass on their hard-earned wisdom in order to save their offspring the grief and suffering they endured when they were young and stupid. At its worst, it was a way for loud-mouthed, opinionated old busy-bodies to get on everyone's nerves by trying to tell people they didn't know how to do things they knew nothing about ad nauseam. However, good advice is always welcome if it comes from a legitimate source. If you want to learn the violin, listen to Yehudi Menuhin, but if you want to change a plug, don't listen to a guy with no eyebrows. Unfortunately, 'Taking advice' is a very un-human trait. Generation after generation decide to 'Do it their own way', which is basically the same way their parents did it, only in more ridiculous clothes.

Parental advice is pretty much ignored by young humans for three reasons:

1. Parents don't know anything because they're old.

2. Grown-ups are obviously doing something wrong because the planet is in such a dreadful state.

3. I want to have sex all the time and you're making it as difficult as possible without chaining me up in a wardrobe and feeding me homework through the keyhole.

To be honest, throughout history, number three was always the big problem. Lesser life-forms on Earth, such as rats and politicians, merely followed a biological imperative and mated with anything that would stay still long enough, whereas humans invented so many rules about mating that it was a miracle any of us got close enough to wave, let alone have sex. However, I digress.

These snippets of wisdom, dear reader, could well save you from a shark-infested ocean of grief, pain and embarrassment (especially the one involving the vacuum cleaner). They are in no particular order, because grief and bleakness tend to arrive haphazardly and unannounced themselves.

General Advice

Don't keep anything radioactive in your pants. Women find genitals that glow in the dark strangely disturbing for some reason.

Don't, under any circumstances, put your head in anything that has **HEAD REMOVER** written on it, or you could end up like my old friend Shorty 'No-Head' Wainright.

If your girlfriend has her hair done, never, ever tell her you liked it better the way it was before.

Don't have silicon breast implants ... unless you're a woman.

Don't head out to sea on a windsurfer until you've learnt to turn round.

Don't ever think a cheap second-hand parachute with a sign on it saying 'ONLY USED ONCE' is a bargain.

Never give an Australian your address because he'll come and live with you for ever.

Avoid using the phrase 'I don't think you've got the nerve to pull that trigger' when someone is pointing a gun at you.

Don't get into a bollock-kicking contest with Vinnie Jones. Not even if he lets you go first.

Learn to distinguish between liquorice and high-tensile safety rope before going on a space walk.

TASTY

NOT TASTY

If a Rottweiler starts humping your leg ... fake an orgasm.

Never put a certain part of your anatomy into a household appliance. Not even the hoover.

If you get stuck in a bumper-to-bumper traffic jam, and you want to save money, turn off your engine and let the guy behind push you.

Don't go to a restaurant where the napkins are made of better material than your jacket.

If you ever end up owning a pet shop, teach all the parrots to say 'I miss my little brother'. You'll sell a lot more that way.

If you lend someone a fiver and never see them again, it was worth it.

Don't go for a haircut when you're drunk.

If someone steals your car, make sure you get their registration number.

If you're driving in LA and the smog gets so bad you can't breathe, simply crash the car on purpose and suck on the air bag until help arrives.

Don't play frisbee in a dog pound.

Always get married in the morning; that way, if it doesn't work out, you haven't ruined the whole day.

NEVER 'EARD OF 'IM MATE...

Don't do what I did and lend a friend three thousand pounds for plastic surgery. Now I can't recognize him.

If you want to find out whether someone is stupid or not, tell them a light year is a year that has 40 per cent less calories than a regular year. If they say 'Really?', they're stupid.

Always remember, most kinds of trouble start off as fun.

Don't try to understand Einstein's Theory of Relativity. Relativity is like an erection, the more you think about it, the harder it gets.

At a party, don't hide in the fridge for a laugh.

Don't force your head into a saucepan and pretend to be a Dalek to amuse a kid. They only start laughing when you can't get it off.

EXTERMINATE
EXTERMINATE

Always remember, beauty's in the eye of the beholder, but so is ugliness.

If a woman tells another woman that she looks a million, she doesn't mean dollars she means years old.

Don't go scuba diving with a friend who's greedy, 'cos if your air supply gives up at ninety feet, he'll be going 'No, you can't have any of this, this is mine.'

Never let a pissed mate sort your back out by doing something he saw an osteopath do on telly.

And girls, it's OK to laugh in the bedroom, but don't point while you're doing it.

Never buy sushi out of a vending machine.

If you hear the toilet flush and a child's voice going 'Uh, oh', it's already too late.

Never shake an iguana.

Don't test a mains lead with your tongue.

If you're going to use an aerosol with anything dodgy in it, it'll have instructions telling you what to do if you get it in your eyes. Read this BEFORE you use it, 'cos once you've got an eyeful you won't be able to see a bloody thing.

If you're swimming in a lake in Africa, and two crocodiles grab your arms up to the shoulder, clap your hands together sharply and that should stun them.

Advice About Sex

It's always tricky giving advice to people about sex just in case they suddenly look at you all icky and go 'You don't really do that, do you?' Whatever, I've never been one to avoid a challenge through fear of embarrassment. Look at my career for god's sake. So, here goes. Advice about sex.

They say that there is one perfect partner for everyone on the planet. Unfortunately, 99 per cent of the male population is convinced it's Claudia Schiffer, so I wouldn't want to be her. Well, maybe just for one night ... Whatever, on with the advice.

There are a number of things you should never do during sex:

Women, you should never

Answer the phone and chat.

Eat.

Look at your watch.

File your nails.

File your tax returns.

Read the paper.

Talk about marriage (especially on a first date).

Fall asleep and snore.

Men, you should never

Answer the phone and tell someone what you're doing.

Blow your nose.

Whistle.

Think that, to be a winner in the sex stakes, you have to finish first all the time.

Call someone else to see if they want to join in.

Visibly fumble with the remote control for the camcorder.

Chew her underwear.

Shout a running commentary about what you're doing to your friends across the street.

Try to get her to do that thing her sister did that really turned you on.

Not Before 30

My last words on the advice front are in a format that became popular in men's magazines of the late twentieth century. Normally, they would give you a list of things you should have done before you reached the point in your career when you could afford to buy the magazine in the first place. No one in the world has ever accomplished all the things these magazines suggested they should have before the age of thirty. If they had, they'd either be dead, or too bizarre to talk to. Therefore, I've compiled a list of 101 things you should definitely NOT do before the age of thirty. If there is anyone out there that has done more than fifteen of these things and survived, please don't get in touch. I scare easily.

1. Commit suicide.
2. Attempt to remove your own appendix with a potato peeler.
3. Try to convince a group of children that you can speak Venusian.
4. Repeatedly perform the kiss of life on someone in a restaurant who doesn't need or want it.
5. Join a religious sect.
6. See if your goldfish can live in lager.

7. See if you can live in lager.

8. Apply for a job as a traffic warden.

9. Save up for a rainy day but spend it on beer every time it rains.

10. Threaten an American policeman with a plastic machine-gun in Miami for a laugh.

11. Suck fog through a sock.

12. Base your life around aromatherapy.

13. Watch afternoon TV.

14. Impersonate bacon frying at parties.

15. Do graffiti on the back of a Hell's Angel's jacket while he's wearing it.

16. Sellotape a drunken friend to the ceiling.

17. See how much you can keep in your head by pushing things into your ears.

18. Learn to play a harmonica with your nose.

19. Gargle with Swarfega.

20. Attempt to fix your television by sticking a coat hanger in the back while it's turned on.

21. Tell people about your belly-button fluff collection.

22. Eat tofu.

23. Try to enlarge your penis with a vacuum-cleaner attachment.

24. Learn to play the riff from 'Smoke on the Water'.

25. Do an open-mike spot at a comedy club with improvised material based on the previous act.

26. Play poker with someone called 'The Professor'.

27. Stick your face in a blender.

28. Stick your face TO a blender

29. Vote for a political party that you think has all the answers.

30. Go on a fun run.

31. Fill your best friend's shoes with very old yoghurt.

32. Inject bean curd into your eyes.

33. Ask your girlfriend if she thinks there's some genetic reason for the fact that she's not as cute as her sister.

34. Stick your tongue in a mains socket for a bet.

35. Forget to turn up for a date with Claudia Schiffer.

36. Sing karaoke.

37. Retire.

38. Have your teeth pierced.

39. Buy some drugs in a club toilet from a guy called Stretch.

40. Have sex with a stoat.

41. Put on a fake Swedish accent when visiting the dentist.

42. Become a world-famous rock star, then blow your head off.

43. Pant really hard but look relaxed while waiting in the queue at the post office.

44. Learn to play the bagpipes.

45. Encourage any offspring to take up drumming.

46. Spraymount yourself to a bus.

47. Think people are interested in your dreams.

48. Take up dribbling as a hobby.

49. Stand on the central reservation of the M1 and spin until you're too dizzy to stand up.

50. Buy a car from anyone called Big Vinnie.

51. Have 'Made in England' tattooed on your forehead.

52. Sell both your kidneys to a Far East transplants hospital.

53. Leave school before puberty.

54. Join a street gang in South Central LA.

55. Have lipo-suction on your head.

56. Become a social worker.

57. Rely on trains.

58. Get really fat.

59. Get really thin.

60. Send a chain letter to ten friends.

61. Give your home away and go to live in a yurt in Wales.

62. Find yourself subconsciously 'spotting' a train next time you visit a station.

63. Give up.

64. Wear a garment you wore eight years ago

because it's a bit like something that's in fashion at the moment.

65. Put a Femidom on your head and blow it up to the size of the Albert Hall.

66. Expect to have a conversation on the Internet that doesn't involve computers.

67. Smear your ankles with goose fat and do a sponsored, barefoot bungee jump.

68. Try to ride a bike with your right hand on the left handgrip.

69. Win a Blue Peter badge ... and wear it.

70. Gather all your friends in one room, announce that you've won the lottery and inform them

that you won't be speaking to them any more because they're all scum.

71. Decide that riding a unicycle is the coolest thing in the world.

72. Attempt to eat a live walrus.

73. Learn to juggle in order to amuse people and be popular at parties.

74. Try to chat up a girl across a crowded room by blinking obscenities in Morse code.

75. Go out with someone who has more problems than you.

76. Actually swallow the purple pill that a guy called Stretch sold you in the toilets.

77. Win a gurning competition just by standing in the audience.

78. Go white-water rafting on an inflatable banana.

79. Go on holiday with someone in an attempt to patch up a romance.

80. Try a Fat Only diet for six months and die of grease.

81. Give up your career in order to gain a PhD in Welsh. (If you live in Wales, substitute Albanian.)

82. Discover that you know ALL the words to 'American Pie'.

83. Believe an election promise.

84. Try to potty train your cat.

85. Go to a boxing club in a pink tracksuit and pretend to be Anneka Rice.

86. Tell everyone that Liverpool Football Club asked you to be their new striker but you couldn't be bothered.

87. Discover that you have to fake an orgasm during a bout of self-gratification.

88. See how long you can leave the gas cooker on before lighting it safely.

89. Get married before you've found someone you like.

90. Try to chat someone up in a James Cagney voice.

91. Sit down to reflect on your greatest achievement to date and discover that it was learning to blow your own nose.

92. Fail to discover the difference between being tired and being bone-idle.

93. Convince yourself that your best friend won't really mind if you only sleep with his girlfriend the once.

94. Drain all the blood out of your body to see how it feels.

95. Ask your bank manager for a loan while wearing a lime-green chicken suit.

96. Invent a game called 'Pubic Dares' and demonstrate it to your friends by setting fire to your crotch.

97. Spill your guts on an Oprah Winfrey-type show.

98. Actually believe that the title 'Financial Adviser' isn't a euphemism for 'Insurance Salesman'.

99. Look like you're forty.

100. Feel like you're forty.

101. Read this.

Advice on Fun Things to Do in Your Car

Paint the words 'HELP ME' in blood-red paint, with your hand, on the back window of your car and see how far you can drive without being stopped by the police.

Drive around and put every stray cat you see on the back seat of your car. After about five, things should get interesting.

Stop and pray to roadkill.

Forget to wind down the window during a drive-by shooting.

Employ a life-sized model of a Tyrannosaurus Rex as a hood ornament.

Enter a stock-car race and insist on towing a caravan round the track. For added fun, your bank manager should be in the caravan.

Connect your brake lights to your horn so that every time you brake, you hoot the car in front.

Fill your car with helium. Stop regularly to ask for directions.

Play a tape of a human heartbeat very loudly when you stop at traffic lights. Stare at the driver next to you with a manic, wide-eyed expression.

Put a bumper sticker with tiny writing on the back of your car so that people keep crashing into you as they try to read it.

The bumper sticker should read 'Please keep your distance'.

Another jolly bumper sticker is 'KEEP HONKING – I'M RELOADING'. It is only available at Jehovah's Witness Kingdom Halls.

Test your driving skills by trying to parallel park in a small space between two Ferraris ... with your eyes closed.

If you get stopped by a police officer, keep looking at your watch. Then say 'How long is this going to take, because your wife is expecting me'.

Bad Days (Advice on How to Spot Them ...)

We all have good days and bad days. Wouldn't it be useful if you had some way of knowing what kind of day it was going to be. Here are a few hints. You know it's going to be a bad day when ...

... Bruce Willis gets into the lift wearing a dirty tee shirt.

... You get so pissed that your head's spinning round and you know you're just about to throw up and you have to apologize to all your friends and ... pull over on to the hard shoulder.

... When the back of your coat gets caught in the Tube doors as you're getting OFF.

... When you wake up somewhere official-looking in Saudi Arabia ... with a HANGOVER and a road cone.

... When you turn up for a party in your normal clothes and then discover it's fancy dress ... but no one notices.

... A beautiful foreign female secret agent thrusts a package into your hands as she's escaping from a group of gunmen and tells you to bring it to her in her bedroom that night … but you lose it.

… Aliens abduct you and ask you to have sex with one of their females and two weeks later their whole race dies of the clap.

… Just when you've finally got a date with the woman of your dreams God appears and tells you you're the chosen one and you have to wander the Earth in sackcloth and ashes trying to convince a bunch of unbelieving bastards that you're the new Messiah. (I hate it when that happens.)

... Keith Chegwin turns up at your house at seven in the morning and tells you you're live on breakfast TV and you can't find anything heavy to hit the bastard with.

... You have a whirlwind romance, you're in the middle of a marriage ceremony but, as you're putting the ring on, you notice she's got webbed fingers.

... My biggest nightmare is waking up one morning and discovering that all this is a dream and I really do live on Starbug.

Children

Throughout history, children have always been the most frightening individuals on the planet. I went to school with them as a kid and they were frightening then; but, as an adult, they can really screw you up. This is because they are so honest and also so inquisitive. There's a secret society that's trying to save adults from children. They leave important messages on everyday objects. I have a lighter with a sticker on it that reads 'Keep out of reach of children.' That's some seriously good advice 'cos they will mess you up. It's OK when they're little, they just pull your hair and crap on your trousers but as soon as they can talk, they start asking THOSE questions. The ones you can't answer. The ones that make you feel like a total blockhead because you know you should be able to answer them. They're only asking because they think you know everything, and, of course, you let them think that. It makes you feel good. But all of a sudden they come out with something like: 'You know clouds? ... how do they stay up in the sky? ... why don't they come down to the ground?' And you smile and nod wisely, you pat them on the head and say 'Well, you see, clouds are made of water vapour, and water vapour is denser than air, so ... SO WHAT THE HELL ARE THEY DOING UP THERE? THEY SHOULD BE DOWN HERE FOR CHRIST'S SAKE!'

117

And you realize you haven't got a clue. Why DO they stay up there? You must have been bunking off school the day they did clouds 'cos you have no idea whatsoever. And while you're worrying about that, they hit you with a whole bunch of other impossible questions ... Where does wind start? ... Where do all the flies go in winter? ... How does a microwave oven make things hot? ... If iron doesn't float, why don't all the ships sink? ... Where does a tree get all its wood from? ... Why is the sky always blue? ... Who wrote the Bible? ... Where do the songs on the radio go when you turn it off? ... How come we can see through glass if it's so hard?

Kids can ask questions like this for hours on end, and they expect you to answer them because you're their dad and you're supposed to be clever. You thought you were until a seven-year-old kid started asking all these ridiculously sensible questions. So you come up with that tired, grown-up excuse: 'Well ... I could tell you son, but you wouldn't understand, you're too young. Ask me in a couple of years' time.'

So they wait a couple of years. But by then they've started to get intellectual: If Jesus was Jewish, why's he got a Mexican name? ... When you pour out boiling water, why does it sound different to cold water? ... If car tyres wear out, where does all the rubber go?

So many perfectly reasonable questions ... and you can't answer any of them. All of a sudden, you realize that you don't know anything. So you ask your mates, and you realize they don't know anything either. You have to reconcile yourself to the fact that you're gonna go through life as THE GUY THAT KNOWS NOTHING ABOUT ANYTHING. You'll have recurring nightmares about your kid at school being asked by his friends: 'What's your dad like?' and he says 'Oh, he doesn't know anything.' But it doesn't end there. They get a bit older and they start coming out with all the really personal shit:

'Why did you start smoking if you knew it was bad for you? ...'

'Why do you call people idiots when you're driving when you don't even know them? ...'

'Why do you drink alcohol at parties if you know it's gonna make your head hurt in the morning?'

And you suddenly realize that you asked your father all the same, stupid questions when you were a kid and you suddenly understand what you must have put him through. So you phone him up, and you say sorry for the endless, stupid questions you asked him when you were a kid ... and he says 'Yeah, fine ... but what is it with the clouds? How the hell DO they stay up there?'

PART FOUR

PLANET EARTH:

THE BIRTHPLACE OF
MANKIND AND LAGER

Naturally, no chronicle of the human race and its doings would be complete without some mention of the place in which we do our doings. However, I have to be honest: although I'd love to write about the fabulous rose-red city of Petra, I haven't been there, so I can't. However, I have been to a couple of places. Here are my thoughts on them, for what they're worth. If they provide you with concise and insightful information about the world we live in ... you should get out more.

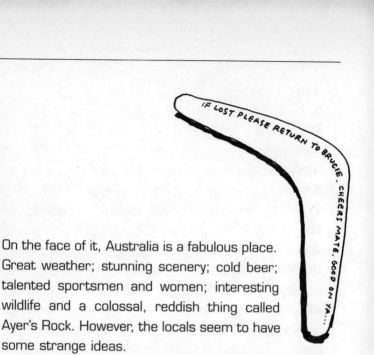

On the side of the boomerang: IF LOST PLEASE RETURN TO BRUCIE. CHEERS MATE. GOOD ON YA...

Australia

On the face of it, Australia is a fabulous place. Great weather; stunning scenery; cold beer; talented sportsmen and women; interesting wildlife and a colossal, reddish thing called Ayer's Rock. However, the locals seem to have some strange ideas.

Can someone explain something to me: Australian Rules? ... What rules? There aren't any. It's just a fight with a ball. It's the scariest game in the world. And the height they jump, call me perceptive, but if you can jump like that, I'm sorry, but someone in your family has been overly intimate with a kangaroo, and believe me, it's not easy. They can't half kick.

American football players think British rugby players are insane for playing without the sort of armour they themselves use. If they ever witnessed the carnage of an Australian Rules match, they'd probably pass out.

Australians have a unique culture but there are a number of salient questions about it that need answering.

Tell me, is there such a thing as UNFAIR dinkum?

Wagga Wagga? Is it really so great they named it twice?

I remember the first time I saw a guy with a didgeri-doo. I remember thinking 'There is no way I am ever going to mess with a guy that can play that without passing out.'

And they've got some seriously big fish over there. Call me a wuss, but if I go fishing, I don't want to catch ANYTHING that's bigger than me. And they've got an entire species of practical-joke spiders over there called redbacks. These antisocial, multi-legged individuals hide under the toilet seat and bite your arse when you're at your most vulnerable. Then they run off, sniggering. There is virtually no animal in Australia that won't bite you given half the chance. I was doing a TV show over there, and a game warden gave me a fluffy little koala bear to hold. The bastard bit me! Even the teddy bears try to eat you in Australia.

Then there's 'Bush tucker'. That's some kind of screwed-up cuisine. These guys go out in the bush, dig maggots out of a tree and eat them! They think it's dead clever that they can survive in the middle of nowhere by eating things that, if we saw them in England, we'd call the police. I'll tell you what's clever: Take some bloody sandwiches.

Australia's massive but everyone lives round the edge. Probably because the middle bit's so shite. I went to Alice Springs on a shoot once and believe me, this place is on the outskirts of nowhere. I have to tell you, *Mad Max* wasn't a film, it was a documentary. They don't play darts in the pubs there, they have 'Punching each other in the head' competitions. The women aren't allowed to join in though. They have to content themselves with dwarf throwing. When I was there they came up with a new game called Red-Dwarf throwing. Apparently, I would have broken the record if I hadn't hit a barn on my way down.

They say there are more venomous creatures than non-venomous in Australia, so it's not the safest place in the world. However, if it's kangaroo-skin slippers you want, there's no finer place in the world.

A WEE DRAM

Scotland

Scotland worries me for a number of reasons. Firstly, it's the only country in the world whose national dress includes a concealed knife in the sock. There's a clue there surely. And the kilt. Contrary to what some people might say, the kilt is THE most masculine item of clothing in the entire universe. Scotsmen wear kilts with nothing underneath so that they can shag anything that moves as rapidly as possible without having to mess about with zips and buttons. And when I say anything that moves, I mean anything.

And the sporran, where did that come from? I'll tell you: the sporran represents a mad badger clamped to the genitals. Apparently, in ancient times, when a Highlander was feeling a bit peckish and fancied frying up a quick badger, he would locate a set and dangle his genitals outside the entrance as bait while regaling the badger with taunts such as 'Oh, what a crappy badger you are and no mistake.' This would incense the badger, who would come flying out of the set, teeth first, and clamp itself on to the Highlander's genitals. The clansman would give a triumphant whoop, wipe the tears from his eyes and run, groin first into the nearest tree to stun the badger who would then be prised off with a concealed knife and end up roasting over a cow-pat fire. Guys, next time you see a sporran, I guarantee you'll go 'EEESH'.

The kilt is also used as a method of challenging an opponent. That's why it looks like a girl's skirt. It's to put the opposition at ease until you've bitten their lungs out. You can just see a Scotsman, kilt flapping in the breeze, in the middle of New York. Strolling through the rougher district of Spanish Harlem, just waiting for a Hispanic street gang to notice him, whereupon he'll stop, indicate his kilt with a nonchalant wave of his hand and say 'Oh, aye ... and what are ye gonna' do about it then?'

I've seen a lot of street fights in my time, but when the ambulance arrives, the guy they pick up is always a sporran-free zone.

NEVER, EVER, mess with anyone wearing a kilt.

Three unconnected events recently prompted me to reassess the way I look at London. One was the fact that I was returning from the relative peace of the countryside, two was that I had been reading Dante's *Inferno*, and three was a sudden spell of hot weather. I suddenly realized that London IS Hell.

There are seven distinct levels to the purgatory that is London. The outer level is in the form of a massive, black ring that circles the boiling core. Some call this ring Acheron, but most refer to it as the M25. Around this ring, the souls of the damned hurtle in a chaos of speeding, crashing metal in a desperate attempt to reach the inner levels, driven by the erroneous belief that things will be better there. They are not.

The air throughout the London

FLY! FLY!

129

inferno is perpetually tainted with noxious fumes and choking vapours that scarify the lungs and tear the eyes. Filthy, black, flapping shapes fill the air, diving amongst the throng to scavenge for scraps or to die messily beneath the crushing wheels of speeding cars as they swerve to avoid the black killer cabs that plough relentlessly through the streets, slaying all in their path.

A black-hearted river runs through the centre of perdition. A stinking, swirling torrent crossed at intervals by crumbling bridges beneath which God's bankers swing on creaking ropes.

There is a stark, bony figure on one side of this river, dressed all in black. He approaches lost souls who are encouraged to press a silver coin into his skeletal hand, whereupon he will furnish them with a copy of the *Big Issue.*

The next level is a maze of soot-grimed tunnels buried deep in the earth. Here, tormented shades are crushed and jostled. Forced into metal cylinders and left stewing in dark, rat-infested tunnels as all hope drains from their wretched spirits and darkness seeps into their very souls.

The third level is a scattered domain. Here and there throughout the inferno you will find the piteous huddles of those whose sin was the sin of penury. These wretches skulk in filthy corners in pools of excrement muttering forlorn supplications to any that will listen. No one ever does. There is no compassion in Hell.

Then there is the dread level of the hedonists. This

is a vast warehouse into which thousands upon thousands of souls are herded and crushed. They are fed a demonic potion that dooms them to dance until they drop to the rhythmic pounding of Hell's generators under the coruscating flashes of the chthonic welders who are forever busy, building the hurtling metal boxes in which the mad, teeming souls of the outer level are to be imprisoned.

The next tier is but a room. This is the level of the malcontents. Those who are dissatisfied with their state of mind. These wretches are fated to sit around a table and listen to the interminable babble of nonsense they generate as demons feed them an endless stream of tainted drugs through their noses. The room resounds with the vapid details of grand schemes that will come to nought and impassioned entreaties for some of the good stuff that made them feel OK for twenty seconds all those years ago.

Yet another level is known as Oxford Street where diverse souls are damned to search endlessly for something worth having at a reasonable price. If they succeed, they will attain salvation. No one yet has.

The cheap-thrill seekers have a level all to themselves, for their title is in itself a paradox. In certain red-hued back streets, sad individuals scurry from shadow to shadow, regaled from dark doorways by the strident entreaties of painted succubi, seeking a glimpse of beautiful female flesh and a decent drink. They will find neither, but are eternally doomed to pay dearly for weak cider and cellulite under the watchful gaze of a massive demon called Vinnie, who carries a credit-card swiper and a lead pipe.

The bearers of false witness, the uncaring and the power-hungry are banished to a large hall. Here they are dressed in ill-fitting grey suits, separated into opposing factions and ranged opposite each other in staggered tiers. Ordered thusly, they are doomed for ever to argue across the dividing floor with no side giving an inch or ever agreeing on anything. This is one of the saddest levels of the inferno.

There are subsidiary torments for those who finally manage to escape the confines of the endless ring around purgatory. Once inside, they are doomed to drive down endless narrow streets patrolled by sour-faced demons in uniform whose only purpose is to prevent these exhausted, tormented souls from ever stopping.

Those desperate enough to attempt a halt are cruelly hobbled with heavy iron boots and left there, immobilized for eternity.

There is a freezing hell for those guilty of the sin of growing old. They are banished to concrete towers of ice with nothing but a constant stream of final reminders to burn for fuel. However, they have no matches and can only ignite the bills when young demons slip fire bombs through their letter boxes. These sad souls are dying from the cost of living.

Throughout the London inferno you will find the thief dens. Here, anything left unattended for more than five seconds will disappear forever. And in the streets, watches and jewellery are torn from the bodies of any foolish enough to be so adorned, by drug-crazed imps.

Those that escape the clawed snatchers are stopped by the roving officers of perdition in their stark black uniforms, who will rummage roughly through your soul for any sign of guilt. They rarely fail to perceive some evidence of culpability and regularly drag screaming souls off to their noisome dungeons where a peculiar kind of gravity causes their prisoners to fall endlessly down stairs and walk into doors.

Another stratum awaits the wannabes and poseurs who will find the gates to their imagined heaven barred by a large devil in a tuxedo who will repeat endless catechisms about a mythical list upon which their names do not now, and never will, appear. Their pathetic pleas involving 'obvious mistakes' and 'don't you know who I am?'s forever fall on deaf and dispassionate ears.

There is also a two-dimensional level to the inferno as thin as cheap paper. Here, everything is black and white and souls are ritually torn apart in print as punishment for the sin of being interesting. It is here that every bad photograph anyone has ever had taken will appear. The demons that run this level of purgatory smell of smoke and whisky and suffix everyone's names with their incorrect age and marital status. Minos, minus the charm.

This is the London Inferno. Abandon hope all ye who enter here.

Naturally, this chronicle would be woefully inadequate without a literary alleluia to that diadem of cities, the centre of the known universe, the spiritual home of chirpy banter: Liverpool. I owe a great deal to Liverpool. So much so, that the fact that Liverpool owes me two bikes; one car; two videos and a tele; a set of plug spanners; a wallet from Greece; a leather duffle-bag full of dirty washing nicked from Liverpool station and a bag of assorted groceries, means nothing.

Nil, nada, zilch, when set against the immeasurable benefits I gleaned, survival-wise, from an upbringing in Toxteth. They say 'See Naples and die.' Such was the beauty and cosmopolitanism of Naples, that, once you'd seen it, you'd pretty much seen it all. There's a similar saying about Toxteth, but it has a far more literal meaning. The only reason the Mersey runs through Liverpool is that, if it walked, it'd get mugged.

There used to be a saying about Liverpool: 'If it's not bolted to the ground, it'll get nicked.' This is totally unfair. We had a family car for years that was never stolen. It was never driven either. It was bolted to the ground.

Forgive me, Liverpool, you know I'm only joking. I love you. Although some of your cuisine can leave a bit to be desired. There's a meal in Liverpool called scouse. It's made of whatever happens to be left over from last night's scouse plus an extra potato. That's why scousers are called scousers.

Scousers are nothing, if not resourceful. A friend of mine came up with a strong contender for the 'Worst Idea Ever' award. I can sum it up in three words: Rat's milk cheese. He figured out that rats were cheap and easy to breed, so he started a rat farm in his bedsit, milked them and made cheese in his bath. And it worked, and he got people to try it and they said it was all right, then he told them it was rat's milk cheese and they threw up on his carpet. He couldn't face the idea of cleaning so much sick off the carpet, so he just sprayed the puddles with rubber solution and peeled them off which gave him another idea so he phoned a practical joke company and is now spending the millions he made from inventing fake rubber sick.

And if you believe that, you're not a scouser.

PART FIVE

HOW TO BE
REALLY ANNOYING

Some people seem to have a natural talent for being incredibly annoying. It's like a weird talent they possess. Something that gives them the ability to wind you up with a subtle glance or a throwaway comment and sometimes, you just wish you could annoy them back but you can't. You're just too nice. The following section might be of use if you ever want to really annoy someone. I'm not advocating that you do this. Far from it. In fact, if you only did half the things that follow, you would swiftly become the most hated person in the known universe. Instead, use this as a guide to what not to do if you want to have friends.

Reply to everything someone says with 'That's what you think.'

Lend your car to a friend and then report it as stolen for a laugh.

Write 'X equals buried treasure' all over someone's road-maps.

Finish everything you say with the words 'In accordance with the prophecy'.

Always pay for everything in five-pence pieces.

If you're going to a party, collect a bunch of winos, take them with you, tell the host they're a hot new band and leave them there.

Phone a tabloid newspaper and make an appointment to show them photographs of their editor in bed with two transvestites. Phone back soon after and cancel the appointment, saying you've accepted a very generous offer from their main rivals.

If you're doing a presentation to important clients, occasionally bob your head like a parakeet.

If you know any fitness freaks, tell them they're looking tired and ill every time you see them.

Stand on the pavement and point a hair-dryer at
passing cars to see if they slow down.

Go to a public demonstration of faith healing,
get up on stage and tell the guy you're deaf.
When he lays on the hands to heal you,
scream and blunder around the stage saying
you've gone blind as well. If he grabs you
again, collapse and say you've lost the use of
your legs.

During a learned lecture, occasionally snigger and mutter 'Yeah, right' in a sarcastic tone.

Anytime someone tells a joke, say 'Oh, god, not that old chestnut.'

If you're on a jury, catch the defendant's eye, grin and draw your finger across your throat.

If someone dials a wrong number and calls you by mistake, have a long and involved discussion with the caller about the person they ask for, saying how worried you are about their 'little problem' and how you hope you can keep the police out of it. If the caller thinks you're a restaurant and wants to order a takeaway, take the order.

If you're on holiday, introduce yourself to the most obnoxious people you meet, using the name of someone you don't like. Give them this person's address and invite them and their families to come and stay for as long as they want to.

Go to a restaurant and order a rare steak. When it arrives, send it back and ask them to cook it just a little more. Do this about thirteen times until you can finally demand to see the manager and ask him how on earth he expects you to eat such an appalling lump of inedible charcoal.

Any time anyone coughs, however slightly, grab them and insist on performing the Heimlich manoeuvre for at least five minutes, no matter how much they protest.

If you meet a fascist bigot who goes on and on about the homeless, and how they should pull themselves together and get jobs, simply burn his house down while he's playing golf and see how he likes it.

When no one's looking, move the throwing line back a foot in a serious darts pub. Then, sit back and take the mickey out of all the players for being so useless. (Tip: wear dart-proof clothes.)

Stand behind a crowd of people playing a triv machine in a pub and shout out all the wrong answers in a very insistent voice.

Sit on a bus or train with an unlit cigarette in your mouth and a lighter in your hand for the whole journey. See how many officials and fellow passengers you can get to point out the NO SMOKING signs while you point out that you're not, in fact, smoking.

Stand by a zebra crossing and every time a car stops, walk off. (I know how annoying this is, people do it to me all the time.)

Lend a neighbour your lawn-mower, then, two weeks after he's returned it, ask for it back repeatedly. If he sees you using it, insist that you lent him your spare one and keep demanding that he return it.

If someone you know greets you in the street, pretend not to know them and threaten to call the police if they don't leave you alone.

Shame a whole load of cowardly friends into signing up for a charity parachute jump with you. Then, don't turn up.

Win the lottery, buy a beautiful castle ... and have it stone-clad. Having said that, just winning the lottery will probably be enough to annoy most people.

Make up insulting acronyms for all your friends' names, and tell them. PAT could stand for Pompous Arrogant Twat; JOHN could be Jerk Off Horrible Nose; DEL Drives Everyone Loopy; MARTIN Married A Right Tart In Norwich. The possibilities for annoying everyone you know are endless.

Go round knocking on people's doors and asking them if they're happy with their washing powder.

Buy one of those watches with a built-in TV remote control, go round to a friend's house during the cup final and change channels every time it looks like someone might score.

Keep buying your girlfriend really nice clothes that are one size too small. (This is a perfect recipe for loneliness or, in extreme cases, death.)

Anytime you visit someone's house, insist on tuning in their TV and hi-fi 'properly', make a complete mess of it, then leave.

Chain-smoke cheap cigars in a vegetarian restaurant.

Tell everyone you've given up cigarettes but carry on smoking theirs.

Whistle a loud, repetitive, tuneless song any time you're in a queue.

Slip a handful of banana-flavoured condoms into a married friend's jacket pocket.

Insist on drinking large brandies every time someone gets a round in. Just before it's your round, go to the toilet for twenty minutes. If you finally have to get them in, buy yourself a half of lager, then go back to large brandies when someone buys the next round.

Every time someone bends over near you, blow a raspberry.

AND FINALLY, THE ULTIMATE ANNOYING THING YOU CAN DO TO ANYBODY:

When someone stops their car at the lights, run over, smear dirty, slimy soapsuds all over their windscreen, spread it around with a filthy sponge and demand payment for the service. If they refuse, scream abuse and make obscene gestures with your squeegee.

PART SIX

FOOD AND
HOW TO DO IT

They say an army marches on its stomach. They say the way to a man's heart is through his stomach, which, vis-à-vis bayonets, has a certain, cold-steel, ring of truth. However, enough inane babble. Food. Where would we be without it? Probably out looking for it. They say a civilized person is only four missed meals away from savagery, and you can't argue with 'They', simply because you might be one of them. While we're on the subject. Who is it that decides who 'They' are. Who is this 'Them' that choses the 'They' that seem to have an opinion on everything under the sun. But, more importantly, what's for lunch? Which brings us rather clumsily on to the subject of this chapter. Food and how to do it.

Along with sex, food has always been one of the two driving passions of the human race. Put a hungry man in a room with a roast-beef dinner and a willing girl and his eyes will dart back and forth like a tennis fan on speed while he tries to work out a sexual position that will allow him to eat and have sex at the same time.

Food and sex will always be closely linked. The man that invented chocolate-flavoured condoms was no fool, if you know what I mean.

I am, in fact, an expert with food but sadly, only from the point of view of eating it. The chances of me entering a kitchen and subsequently leaving soon after with a plate of pan-fried scallops on a bed of rocket with balsamic vinegar and shaved Parmesan are pretty slim. In the past, I have cooked meals which melted in your mouth, but that was before I discovered defrosting.

Whatever, no chronicle of the human race would be complete without a selection of recipes that would allow the recipient of this book to create some of the finest dishes in the universe. The human race has produced a number of greats in the art of cooking: Albert Roux, Egon Ronay, Ronald McDonald to name but a few. As the last remaining human in the Universe, it would be my duty to pass on some of the culinary secrets of my ancestors. At the end of the day, it's always best to write about what you know. Here's what I know. Read this chapter and you'll almost believe a pan can fry.

No laughing at the back please.

Glossary of terms

COOKING – To cook something, make it hot for a while. Then it's cooked. It's a doddle. I was amazed too when I found out how simple cooking is.

FOOD – For the sake of clarity and brevity, the word 'food' in this book means anything you can put in your mouth that doesn't kill you. However, there is an exception to this tenet which you'll find in the section on sex.

THE KITCHEN – A mysterious place full of sharp, pointed objects, deadly gas-operated incinerators, things that go 'ping' and a big, cold wardrobe full of beer which is the only true incentive for entering the room in the first place.

Author's note – I didn't fight my way to the top of the food chain in order to eat vegetarian food but, for the many people who prefer this sort of cuisine, I've included a large number of vegetarian recipes which are indicated by the letter V.

Recipes

Here are a few of my personal favourites.

Sugar Puff Sandwiches (V)

Ingredients: 2 slices of bread
a handful of sugar puffs
some butter

Spread the butter on the two slices of bread. Arrange the sugar puffs on the bottom slice, slap the top slice of bread on top and eat.

Food Vindaloo

Ingredients: food
Vindaloo sauce

Cover the food in vindaloo sauce. Microwave it until it explodes. Eat it.

Top-Shelf Oblivion Sorbet (V)

Ingredients: a dash of everything on the top shelf of the medi-lab

Mix the ingredients together and stir into a beaker full of ice. Inform the rest of the crew that you'll see them in a week or two and drink it.

Chilli Sauce Challenge (V)

Ingredients: chilli sauce
      lager

Open a bottle of chilli sauce and a bottle of lager and see how much chilli sauce you can eat before you have to drink the lager.

No-Fish Fondue (V)

Ingredients: little bits of bread on sticks
      brandy
      no fish

Place the brandy in a bowl making sure to include no fish. Dip the bits of bread into the brandy and eat them until all the brandy is gone. Then go to bed.

Can Surprise (Possible V)

Ingredients: a can of food

Remove the labels from a number of cans of food. Select one at random, open it, eat it and try to guess what it is.

Road-Kill Grill

Ingredients: road-kill

Run something over, grill it and feed it to people

Beef Wellington

Ingredients: some beef
               a pair of wellington boots

Slice the beef into two thin steaks. Place them inside the wellington boots and walk around on them for a couple of weeks until they're tender. Then remove the steaks and hide them under the pillow of someone you don't like.

Vegetarian Veal Risotto

Ingredients: veal
            rice

Cook the veal and the rice together, then eat the veal and offer the remaining rice to a vegetarian you don't like.

Curry Sauce

Curry sauce is the basis of all haute cuisine and can only be found in cans with 'Curry Sauce' written on them.

Ingredients: Curry Sauce

Open the can and cover any food you are about to eat with the contents. This will immediately render the food edible and bring you out in a sweat, which is the only way you can tell you are eating a decent meal.

Cocktail Corner

Of course, no gourmet meal could be deemed complete without the correct libation. The following cocktails are all vodka-based and should only be made using VLADIGOOD vodka. This is simply because it is the very best vodka in the universe and nothing whatsoever to do with a lucrative sponsorship deal. So, grab a straw and suck my cocktail.

Slow Comfortable Shrew in the Park

Ingredients: a large shot of premium vodka
(may I recommend VLADIGOOD)
200 ml fresh orange juice
100 ml pineapple juice
a quantity of crushed ice
1 shrew

Pour the orange and pineapple juice over the ice. Let the shrew drink the vodka. Take it to the park and watch it being slow and comfortable while drinking the refreshing fruit drink.

Carvery Ballwangler

Ingredients: a bottle of VLADIGOOD vodka

Drink the delicious, refreshing bottle of VLADIGOOD vodka. Go to a carvery, order the beef and then insist that the chef gives you the sweetbreads as well. The warming effects of VLADIGOOD vodka will do wonders for your dogged persistence and the chef will eventually accede. Congratulations, you and VLADIGOOD have accomplished a worthwhile wangle.

Moscow Mole

Ingredients: 1 bottle of VLADIGOOD vodka
            1 duvet

Drink half the bottle of VLADIGOOD vodka, burrow your way under the duvet like a mole, drink the other half of the bottle and mutter to yourself in Russian.

Screw Driver

Ingredients: 1 bottle of VLADIGOOD vodka
            1 carton of orange
            1 car

Mix the vodka with the orange and pretend you're just drinking fruit juice. This will give people the illusion that you are fit to drive. This is not the case. A bottle of VLADIGOOD vodka is enough to screw any driver. Leave the car behind and get a cab.

PART SEVEN

WHAT THE
HUMAN RACE
IS ALL ABOUT

Some scholars would argue that the best way to judge the human race is by summarizing its greatest achievements and weighing them in the balance. This is obviously nonsense. Leonardo, Galileo, Shakespeare, Mozart, Newton, Einstein et al. were clearly blessed with genius and enriched the lives of millions with their brilliance. However, they had little in common with the majority of the human race. We are not all creative or scientific geniuses. Far from it, in fact, but at some time in our lives, most of us 'Have a go'. This willingness to risk everything to achieve a goal is what, for me, defines the spirit of the human race. It would be easy to applaud those who have 'Had a go' and succeeded, but for me, those that went for it and failed in a spectacular fashion are more worthy of note. More deserving of a niche in the Human Being Hall of Fame, simply because they can make the rest of us feel extremely clever in comparison.

One of the most endearing qualities of Homo sapiens is our ability to do the most unbelievably stupid things. Certain, gifted individuals have stunned the world with their selfless, thoughtless and usually brainless acts of monumental folly and peerless stupidity.

What follows is a brief catalogue of some of the more noteworthy disasters our fellow humans have managed to perpetrate upon themselves. I haven't made them up because I couldn't. No one could. However, I assure you that they are all authentic and reliably reported occurrences that have appeared in respected publications throughout the world. In this section, truth leaves fiction standing in the starting blocks complaining that it didn't even hear the gun.

Bad Idea of the Year

Sometimes, heavy, military transport aircraft need to take off from short runways. If they can't manage this under their own power they will use a JATO (Jet Assisted Take Off) unit, which is a high-powered, solid-fuel rocket. If you somehow came into possession of a JATO, what would you do with it?

Not long ago, the Highway Patrol in Arizona discovered a pile of twisted, charred metal embedded 3 feet into a cliff face, 125 feet above the ground. Their first thoughts were that it must be a light aircraft that had crashed into the cliff but, on further inspection, it turned out to be the remains of a 1967 Chevy Impala. A certain amount of detective work established the likely cause of this rather unusual collision. The driver of the Chevrolet had acquired a JATO and bolted it on to his car. He had then selected a long straight road, accelerated to a reasonable speed and then fired the JATO. This would have caused the Impala to accelerate to 350 mph within 5 seconds, the thrust continuing for at least another 20 seconds. Two and a half miles after ignition the thick rubber marks on the road

surface indicated that the driver had attempted to use the brakes which immediately melted, blowing all four tyres. By this time, any control the driver might have over the rest of the journey was totally insignificant – especially when the car reached a bend in the road and took off. The car flew for about one and a half miles before smashing into a cliff face, 125 feet above ground, where it embedded itself in a crater 3 feet deep. The majority of the driver's remains were not recoverable, although fragments of fingernail and bone were removed from what was believed to be a section of the steering wheel.

No matter how much fun this little adventure might sound, don't try it at home, kids.

Fubble Trouble

Miami, Florida, March 1995. According to the *Newcastle Herald* 22 March 1995, the stunningly named Natron Fubble decided to rob his local delicatessen. Sadly for him, the owner didn't feel like being robbed that day and smashed him in the face with a giant salami, breaking his nose. Fubble legged it and, in a bid to evade capture, hid in the boot of a car. The boot of a car belonging to an undercover police surveillance team. It was five days before he was discovered and released.

No Arm Done

A Mr Rodique caused quite a stir when he left his flat in Hamden, Connecticut. The new tenants were rather upset when they found a pair of neatly dissected human arms under the sink. Mr Rodique was an orthopaedic surgeon who had taken the arms from Yale School of Medicine to practise on at home. While packing he had simply forgotten all about them.

Very Toothsome

Three teeth are not what most people would expect to find in a Galaxy Double Nuts and Raisins bar. Merryl Baker did and complained to Mars. The story was reported in the press. However, when Mrs Baker next visited her dentist, he pointed out that three of her own back teeth were missing. Mrs Baker admitted that she felt a little foolish. (*Retail Newsagent* 18 February 1995)

Making a Bomb

British Nuclear Fuels were a tad surprised recently when they received a fax from a second-hand car dealer called Tom in Idaho, offering them first refusal on a pre-owned nuclear fuel reprocessing plant, complete with instruction manual. Presumably the previous owner was a little old lady who only used it to vaporize the local shops on the way to church.

The American Government were somewhat worried by this turn of events as this is not the sort of equipment they would want gentlemen such as Saddam Hussein to find in their Christmas stocking. Maybe US defence officials should have considered this beforehand, for it was they that sold the equipment to Tom Johansen at the Frontier Car Corral in Pocatello, Idaho in the first place. An official from the Nuclear Regulatory Commission did phone Mr Johansen to warn him that he would not be allowed to export the equipment, which put a bit of a crimp in his day as he had serious interest from both Australia and Japan already.

Anyone fancying a cruise should give the Pentagon a ring, they might sell you one.

A Stirling Performance

Big fun on the set of Mel Gibson's film *Braveheart*. Five hundred extras ended up in hospital after getting a bit carried away during a re-enactment of the battle of Stirling (1297 or thereabouts). The extras were recruited from the Irish Reserve Army and were paid £30 per day to hack away at each other using a variety of weighty implements. The overenthusiasm was blamed on the fact that the Irish Reserves see very little real action and were probably making the best of it.

Most of the injuries were from cuts and bruises, but a few of the less doughty warriors collapsed from sunstroke and dehydration. As if this wasn't enough for the beleaguered antipodean to cope with, the gods of comedy saw to it that a hillside battle had to be reshot when some bright spark noticed that three of the thirteenth-century Celtic warriors were wearing glasses and another scene was scrapped altogether because in the thick of a life and death struggle, all the protagonists were seen to be laughing their heads off.

Level Headed?

A certain Anthony Philip Hicks from Truro in Cornwall decided to demonstrate his enthusiasm for funk pop-sters Level 42 by changing his name to something more befitting a true fan of the band. His new monica is Ant Level Forty Two The Pursuit Of Accidents The Early Tapes Standing In The Light True Colours A Physical Presence World Machine Running In The Family Running In The Family Platinum Edition Staring At The Sun Level Best Guaranteed The Remixes Forever Now Influences Changes Mark King Mike Lindup Phil Gould Boon Gould Wally Badarou Lindup Badarou.

Ant admits that 'Some people might think I am crazy.' Presumably he's referring to his bankers who will have to provide him with a fourteen-foot cheque book.

Batty

During the Second World War the US Air Force captured vast amounts of bats in order to develop a bat bomb. The theory being that the little airborne rodenty things would fly into enemy territory and blow things up with the little bombs they were carrying. After two million dollars of research and development, the only things the bats had managed to destroy were an aircraft hangar and a general's car.

GO FOR IT, TARQUIN!!

King Crustacean

This is surely the finest piece of news this century. Dateline Dover. A girl who had drifted out to sea on a set of inflatable teeth was heroically rescued by a man on a blow-up lobster. You can't even fabricate stories like that.

Alien Tomato

Britain is considering banning a genetically engineered tomato that has been approved for sale in the States.

A Government watchdog is worried that the tomato, containing two 'alien' genes, could spread bacterial disease via their innate antibiotic resistance. Called the Flavr-Savr tomato, it is the fruit of a science and patent battle between Zeneca, an offshoot of ICI, and Calgene, an American company. Sounds ravr luvry.

Incowgnito

An Irish farmer from Monaghan, Ireland is awaiting trial on charges of indecent assault, indecent exposure, incest, buggery, sodomy and bestiality allegedly involving his son, his daughter, an unidentified travelling salesman and what has been described as a 'named dairy cow' by a Court in Dublin. The cow cannot be named to protect the identity of the farmer.

Thunder Box

A 74-year-old man complained that ambulancemen 'laughed their heads off' when they discovered that his severe burns were the result of cleaning his toilet with lighter fuel, then throwing a cigarette into the toilet as he sat on it. Ouch.

Stupid or What?

Four friends from Virginia, USA, being somewhat the worse for wear after a drunken binge, decided to play 'Chicken' by lying between the tracks in front of an approaching freight train, confident that said train would pass harmlessly over them. Unfortunately the train was fitted with a snow-plough.

Bubble Head

Abner Kriller of Albany, Australia was not what you might call a natural multi-tasker and came to grief while attempting to drive and chew gum at the same time. Things were going fine until he blew a huge bubble which burst in his face, blinding him and causing him to miss a bend and drive over a cliff. (*The People* 4 September 1994)

Well Dumb

Picture a farm in Nazlat Imara, two hundred and forty miles south of Cairo. This was the setting for a series of disasters that beggar the imagination. A chicken has fallen down a sixty-foot well. An eighteen-year-old farmer descended into the well to rescue said chicken but succumbed to an undercurrent in the water which pulled him down and drowned him. His brother followed him down the well in a rescue attempt and also drowned. His other brother tried to rescue them both and drowned as well, as did their sister. Two elderly farmers also pitched in and, surprise surprise, yes, they drowned as well.

The bodies of all six were finally pulled out of the well, as was the chicken, which was still alive.

Axe Victim

Ron Newman of Chatham has been sentenced to 140 hours of community service for beating his friend over the head with a guitar. The attack was prompted by his friend persistently playing the wrong chord in the Eagles' song 'Peaceful Easy Feelin'.

Stop Press

Theogenes, a native of Thasos and gladiator in the stable of the cruel prince Thesus has been awarded the 'Hardest Bastard in the World' title. Although he retired around 900 BC, during his career Theogenes killed 1425 men with his bare hands. His speciality was beating his opponents to a pulp with his fists, which were wrapped in leather and studded with metal spikes. This snippet of information appears in this section, not because of Theogenes himself, but in tribute to the monumental error of judgement displayed by the 1424 people that queued up to fight him after he'd ripped the first one apart.

His Number Was Up

According to *The Independent* 11 January 1996, one Maliu Mafua managed to escape from a San Francisco jail. His first deed on the outside was to dial 411 for directory enquiries. Unfortunately he dialled 911 in error and was recaptured when the police turned up and noticed the shirt he was wearing had 'Property of San Mateo County Jail' written across the front which was a bit of a giveaway, even to an American cop.

Nutter

The First World War flying ace Jean Navarre once attacked a German Zeppelin with a bread knife.

A Rude Awakening

One Ken Charles Barger, 47, from Newton, North Carolina, was rudely awakened by the ringing of the telephone next to his bed. He reached out to answer it but unfortunately grabbed the Smith and Wesson he kept next to the bed and fired it into his ear. *The Hickory Daily Record* 21 December 1992 makes no mention of the caller.

Stuck in New Zealand

If you live in Timaru, New Zealand, and your name's Grant Shittit, it's surely only a matter of time before something interesting happens to you. True to form, Mr Shittit was making his way home after a bit of a night out when he felt a sudden urge to lie down and have a nap on a convenient 'bed of moss' he had come across. Unfortunately when he awoke, he discovered said bed of moss was, in fact, fresh cement that had dried overnight and he was well and truly stuck, with only his head protruding. He screamed for help for seventy-two hours until a passing motorist stopped to help what he thought was an injured hedgehog. The local fire service finally freed him with road drills. Grant remarked that 'It was particularly uncomfortable because I'd been sick on myself in the night.' (*Big Issue* 20 March 1995)

Barking Mad

Prison officers in Florida came up with a spectacularly brilliant way to test their new tracker dog. They asked a double murderer called David Graham if he would be willing to pretend to escape while they tracked him with the dog. They even gave him a thirty-minute start. Mr Graham performed admirably; unfortunately, the dog didn't and the prisoner was long gone. (*Sunday Express* 30 October 1994)

A Teeny Error

Saanich, British Columbia. A seventeen-year-old girl in a supermarket tried to pass a cheque for $184. Although she offered two pieces of ID, the cashier called the manager to verify the transaction.

'Is this you?' the manager asked.

'Of course it is,' replied the girl.

'Well,' said the manager 'then you're my ex-wife, but you don't look anything like her.' (*Victoria [BC] Times Colonist* 21 August 1992)

Dopey Voters

In 1970 voters in Picoaza, Ecuador became so confused by an elaborate advertising campaign that they elected a brand of foot deodorant as their mayor.

Flying Frank

Frank Reichalt invented the first parachute and, in 1912, declared that he would test it personally by jumping off the Eiffel Tower. He boasted 'I am confident of success', which was admirable but somewhat misguided. The parachute didn't work.

PART EIGHT

TRANSPORT

Early forms of locomotion relied heavily on the foot. The brighter individuals would use them in pairs. Walking wasn't the simple thing then that it is today and walking schools sprung up across the globe as our ancestors descended from the trees and fell over. The ancient Arctic tundra was rife with hairy, stooped figures with L-plates stumbling around trying to master the intricacies of the 'three-point turn-around' and the insanely difficult 'walking backwards round a corner' manoeuvre.

Early cavemen on the pull would saunter past groups of females and display their walking skills. However, there were always one or two who would get a bit carried away, and a painful head-on collision was often the result.

Mankind felt this need to travel as soon as he realized food didn't just turn up and ask to be considered as the main course for lunch. Instead, it seemed to have an annoying tendency to run away and get on with its own thing, which mostly consisted of not being clubbed, bitten, stabbed or eaten. Early hunting techniques involved skulking around in the underbrush, then, suddenly leaping on a slow-moving shrub and eating its roots before it could get away. Some hunters had such a poor technique that many shrubs did, in fact, escape. These horticultural escapees met up and banded together in a safe enclave that, many years later, came to be known as Kew Gardens.

Eventually, early humans had to reconcile themselves to the fact that, if they wanted anything half-decent to eat, they were going to have to damn well run after it. Some bright individuals noticed that they didn't seem to be catching much. This was mainly because the animals they were chasing could run faster than them. Many a protuberant forehead was scratched in consternation while this problem was considered. Around this time, the bravest human ever to walk the earth strode forward and actually tried to sit on a horse. Think about it. These days we take horse-riding for granted. Anyone can go to a riding school and sit on a docile, knackered old cob while it auto-pilots its way round a few picturesque country lanes but, in prehistory, horses were wild. I take my hat off to the first guy that ever had the nerve to sit on top of a bucking, wild-eyed, nutter of a beast and say to himself 'Now all I've got to do is tame it ... and learn to live with this hoof-print on my face.'

Nothing much changed on the transport front for a few Ice Ages until the invention of the wheel [See INVENTIONS – The Wheel, p196], which led, inevitably, to the development of the McClaren F1. OK, maybe I've skipped a bit here, but what's a few millennia between friends.

During the last years of the twentieth century, satellite global positioning systems allowed the development of in-car navigation computers. I must admit, I find it worrying.

A box sits on your dashboard, and TELLS YOU WHERE TO GO! Your car talks to a satellite, and it always knows exactly where it is. You'll be happily pootling along in your vehicle of choice, and suddenly your car will say (in a perfectly reasonable American accent), 'You didn't want to take that last left, it's much quicker if you go down the High Street and double back through the market.' Excuse me! If I want to get lost I'll get lost. You spend half your life hating smug, back-seat drivers that tell you how much better it would have been if you'd taken some bizarre short-cut through someone's back garden and you swear you'll never drive them anywhere again, and now your car's doing it. And the thing that really annoys me is that you know it's always going to be right. One of the few freedoms we have left is the right to get hopelessly lost in an unfamiliar town and shout about how useless the traffic signs are and what ridiculous one-way systems they've implemented since you were last there. Now they want to take even that away from us.

But I have a solution. We should all get one of these machines ... and wherever it tells you to go ... do the opposite. It'll be a brand new game called 'Get Your Car Lost', because, at the end of the day, you can still drive where the hell you want. The car will be saying 'No, no ... you should have taken that last right, you're going in the wrong direction, driver error, driver error' but you can say 'Hey, I pay for the petrol, I change your tyres ... I'm going MY way, OK?'

Also, what happens if they rearrange a one-way system after you buy the unit? Your car will say cheerily 'Take the next left, and you will be at your destination.' And you'll turn left, straight into a damn great cement truck that's still following those little blue arrows like people used to do when they had minds of their own.

New technology is fine if it just sits in an office and breaks now and then, but if it starts telling me to drive down roads that aren't there any more I am not going to be a happy bunny.

End of rant. What about boats?

Given that two-thirds of the Earth is covered by water, it's hardly surprising that one of mankind's early ambitions was to conquer the great oceans. The theory of floating was closely followed by the theory of sinking and rapidly thereafter by the theory of waving, shouting and drowning but the human race is nothing if not persistent. Persistent AND stupid.

Tribal elders would watch as their bravest warriors disappeared beneath the waves and wander off, muttering about how, maybe, they should have tried the vessel out on a pond first. They would also have decided to have a couple of words with the boat-builder along the lines 'Maybe rock isn't the most efficient building material for boats' and 'You're dead'. Throughout history, designers and builders of boats, planes and starships have always found a lame excuse to miss out on the maiden voyage of their creation. For some reason, the test pilots never seem to question this. If I were a test pilot, I'd ask the inventor if he was confident about the safety of the vehicle. If he answered in the affirmative I'd say 'Well, it's you and me on the maiden run then.'

This concept applies especially to that strangest of all boats, the submarine. Picture the inventor giving his first presentation of the concept to the military. You can just imagine the generals grinning at each other, going 'Yeah, right. Who put you up to this?' Let's face it, a boat that's designed to sink wouldn't immediately strike you as 'Great idea of the week' if you hadn't seen one before. It sounds about as useful as a plane that's designed to crash, or a rifle that's precision-engineered to blow your arms off. Nevertheless, submarines worked, and must have surprised quite a few naval types who probably assumed they were being attacked by exploding fish.

Two hundred years after the takeover (or, more correctly, the repossession) of Hong Kong, much of the world's seaways became unnavigable as myriad boats congesting Hong Kong harbour expanded until they covered the South China Sea and, eventually, the whole of the Pacific, with a log-jam of junks.

The only plus side of this was that you could use the boats to walk halfway round the world.

Man's eternal dream has always been to fly like the birds. Sadly, given that the average human has the aerodynamic properties of a wardrobe full of conkers, this particular ambition had to sit in the corner and twiddle its fingers until technology caught up. The discovery that hot air rises was an early breakthrough. Sadly, a number of rare eagles plummeted to their deaths in hopeless fits of laughter when they realized how long it had taken us to work out something they had been patiently demonstrating for eons.

The hot-air balloon of the Montgolfier brothers brought Paris to a standstill with its effortless ability to go up in the air and then come down again without anyone dying.

'Where can we go in this balloon?' cried the aristocrats.

'Which way is the wind blowing?' cried the Montgolfier brothers.

'West,' cried the aristocrats.

'Well, we can go there,' muttered the Montgolfier brothers, somewhat peeved that a bunch of idiot aristos with bad make-up had been so quick to uncover the Achilles' heel of their great invention. Nevertheless, flying was such a novelty that the idea caught on.

Any new form of transport is always seized upon by the military, who are ever eager to exploit an advantage. The remainder of this section will deal almost exclusively with modes of transport developed or seconded by the military. This is simply, and sadly, because most major innovations in this sphere are funded and abused by a bunch of war-mongering gits whose only interest in transport involves getting to a country as quickly as possible in order to kill the people who live there. Second rant over. Back to history. Tethered balloons were used in the First World War to send quaking privates aloft in order to ascertain enemy movements. We called this 'Aerial intelligence gathering'. The enemy called it 'Target practice' (only in German).

Aviation took off in a big way around this time. Gentlemen aviators took to the skies in biplanes and tri-planes and tried to shoot each other politely, while they swooped, majestically, above the mud and blood-filled trenches of the common soldiers, who were too busy fighting the real war to notice.

After the Second World War pilots tended to be employed on a meritocratic rather than an aristocratic basis. This was simply because aircraft had become so fast. Just prior to the Third World War the air forces of the world realized that they needed to find young-sters with incredible reflexes and stunning hand/eye co-ordination to fly their new jet fighters. A scheme was launched, in conjunction with video-game companies, which would allow the military to record the scores of kids playing virtual-reality flight-simulator games at home, in arcades or on the Internet. The highest-scoring individuals would be inducted into the military to serve as fighter pilots for their country.

The scheme looked perfect on paper. However, the military had failed to take into account the fact that kids who spend all their time playing video games, at home or in arcades, do so because they have no time for the authoritarian regime that schools impose. The last thing they wanted was to join the rigid, disciplinary structure of the military. Unless, of course, the air force would agree to give them their own jet fighter and a private landing strip. Then, maybe, if there was some kind of hassle with a foreign power, they might be willing to kick a little butt. But only if the deal was right. They had the military over a barrel because they both knew there were only a handful of teenaged individuals who were capable of piloting their latest fighters. The kids knew what they were worth. Money and mountain bikes changed hands.

Of course, the first dogfight was a complete farce. The young pilots on both sides had been chatting on the Internet for years. They hacked into the system, dis-abled all the real weapons, and indulged in dogfights for points, rather than lives. At first, the military were up in arms. However, as soon as they realized they weren't losing any expensive aircraft in these battles, they warmed to the idea and, by way of congratulating themselves for having thought of it, gave themselves a pay-rise from the excess funds.

Eventually, a new Geneva Convention decreed that, in future, all air battles would be fought by teenagers, in virtual reality, over the Internet. However, this was not the end of military lunacy.

The Mole Tank of the late twenty-first century was one mode of military transport that signally failed to fulfil its potential. The Joint Chiefs of Staff responsible for the project knew they could attack from the air, from the sea (on or below) and from the land. However, they couldn't attack from UNDER the land. Wouldn't it be useful, they postulated, if they could send troops underground. Troops that could then surface behind enemy lines, and shoot them in the backsides when they weren't looking.

'The basic prerequisite,' said the generals (and here they quoted Caesar, Napoleon and Capone), 'of any successful military operation, is the ability to shoot the enemy in the backside when they're not looking.' Western governments love this sort of jingoistic, tub-thumping dogma. They all said 'Hurrah!' and headed for the subsidized bar.

Thus was the Mole Tank invented. The vehicle was the size of a Greyhound bus and carried fifty highly trained, heavily armed troops who really didn't want to be there. The vehicle was designed to bore its way into the ground from a truck-mounted ramp and travel underground to its destination behind enemy lines, where it would surface, confounding Johnny bad-guy so much that he would be easy to shoot.

The Sinclair C5 of the 1980s was designed to re-volutionize road transport. It was vastly more success-ful than the Mole Tank which, due to a lack of field trials, failed to accede adequately to the simple demands of 'Navigation' and 'Geology'. Sat-nav systems don't work too well underground and even diamond-tipped bore drills have trouble with subterranean gran-ite escarpments. Friction was another important factor that should have merited a tad more consideration.

A number of Mole Tank crews were boiled alive when their air-conditioning units failed to compete with the hull temperature. This particular problem was especially common in the Albanian-built models, which included their revolutionary solar-powered refrigeration option. Any soldiers that expressed their misgivings about the efficacy of a solar-powered device in an underground environment were court-martialled and shot. After all, a soldier is there to obey orders, not to get all clever-clever about technical, boffin stuff.

Of the five hundred Mole Tanks deployed in action, four hundred and sixty-three were finally listed as being 'On indefinite manoeuvres'. This probably means they're still burrowing around somewhere, the half-life of their nuclear fuel being far in excess of the entire life of the crew.

Of the remainder, seven Mole Tanks were found

floating in the middle of the Pacific; fourteen appeared in a variety of mineshafts around the world; four were shot out of a geyser in Iceland; two appeared in Vatican square and had a shrine built around them; one blocked the Channel Tunnel, causing no problems whatsoever to anyone; one burst through the floor of a rave in Ibiza and got a round of applause; two surfaced simultaneously and collided at Venice Beach in LA, where they were sold as a neo-humanist sculpture to Sony for eight billion dollars by a wino; four surfaced at Mount Rushmore in the form of four diamond-tipped, revolving noses. The remaining two actually appeared behind enemy lines, deployed their troops, and achieved a great victory over two one-legged peasants and a guy with a particularly vicious-looking catapult. The project was declared a major success and a further twenty trillion dollars was invested in the enterprise by Congress.

PART NINE

INVENTIONS

When analysing a new invention in order to determine its usefulness and possible impact on the lives of those that will use it, there is a simple question you can ask yourself that will tell you all you need to know. That question is 'What is the problem to which this invention is the solution?' This approach is one of the most useful analytical tools in determining the worth of a given object or idea.

For example, the solution to the problem of how to drive more safely on a road at night is Cat's-eyes. The solution to the problem of how to leave obvious, hard-to-lose messages in an office is Post-it Notes. What on earth is the question to which a 'Pot Noodle' is the answer?

What is the problem to which the solution is a terracotta badger? The solution to the problem of how to look like a total dickhead in public is a bumper sticker on a clapped-out old banger that says 'My other car is a Porsche.' Sadly, this self-imposed banner headline also poses a couple of questions itself: If your other car really is a Porsche, why are you driving that piece of junk, and if you don't have a Porsche and this is an attempt at humour, what does that say about you?

Any innovation can and should be judged using this approach. Interestingly, you can also turn the question around, thus:

SOLUTION: The Lottery.

PROBLEM: How can the Government collect additional taxes to fund needy causes and the arts?

SOLUTION: The Internet.

PROBLEM: How can we get boring computer nerds to stay at home looking at the world through a little screen while we go out and enjoy it firsthand? (Having said this, I'm on the Internet myself, but I still go out, OK!)

The Wheel

The wheel was invented by a prehistoric man who noticed a log rolling down a hill. A stunning new way to revolutionize transport began to form in his hazy, Cro-Magnon mind. Unfortunately, the idea and the log hit him at about the same time, so Man still had to drag things round for another few thousand years until some other bright spark, more fleet of foot and possessing an inherent talent for log-avoidance, came up with the wheel concept.

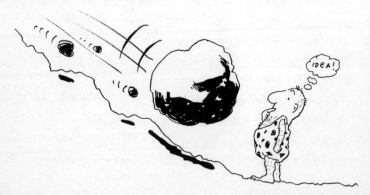

Many things in Man's history have been invented by watching things roll down hills. Someone watching a cart roll down a steep incline into a river came up with the idea of vehicle insurance.

A guy watching his mother-in-law roll down a mountain into an alligator-infested gully spontaneously discovered laughter.

A man sitting on a runaway wagon wore both shoes out during his rapid and somewhat panic-stricken invention of brakes. Skis were invented by a guy who was watching Bjorn 'Long-foot' Svenson going into town, down a snow-covered mountain slope. Of course, Bjorn could have invented skis himself. Unfortunately, the idea never occurred to him because he didn't need them.

So you see, hills were crucial in providing inspiration to early inventors. Perhaps this is why Holland is only famous for tulips and clogs, neither of which are much use on hills.

Many inventions are simply modern revisions of ancient ideas. A goatherd in Sumeria came up with the idea of 'Post-It Goats' many centuries before the office-supply business took off. He would scrawl important messages on the side of goats to remind the villagers of important feast days. Sadly, these feast days normally involved the slaughter of a goat. The phrase 'Don't kill the messenger' was coined at this time. Probably by a goat.

One of my favourite inventions of all time is Potty Putty, because it bounces, it squashes flat, it flows like a liquid, it even picks up newsprint ... but it's completely useless. They even had a nation-wide competition when I was at school to see if anybody could come up with a use for it. To this day, I haven't heard of a winner.

The clockwork radio was an interesting invention, primarily targeted at countries that don't have the luxury of a national grid to supply power. However, this probably means they don't have a local radio station, so all they can hear is the World Service, talking a bunch of gibberish in a foreign language. Great idea though. I'm just waiting for the clockwork car. Unfortunately, you'd probably have to be Arnold Schwarzenegger's big brother in order to wind it.

2217 saw the introduction of the No-Grav flying helmet – a piece of high-tech headgear that allowed people to float about, hanging from their helmets. This wasn't quite as painful as it sounds. However, there were some teething problems with the sports model, which had such fast acceleration that a number of people had their heads ripped off and shot into space. This model was discontinued and is now a much sought-after collector's item, especially by people in unhappy marriages who are looking for that 'special' birthday gift.

Youngskin

Invented in 2165 and touted as the ultimate cosmetic, Youngskin could give anyone the skin of a child. Unfortunately, the child involved tended to suffer somewhat and the process was outlawed twenty minutes after its launch.

Real Virtual Reality

Hyped as the 'Ultimate Experience', Real Virtual Reality was launched by an East End software company in 2109. Vastly expensive, it claimed to allow computer users to leave their consoles and enter a Real Virtual World that was indistinguishable from the real world. It proved a best seller for many months until people noticed a marked increase in computer types, wandering around the city streets, poking things, and feeling strangers' faces in a state of abject wonder.

Dark

The speed of light has always been an important constant in Physics. However, in 2137, Magnus Sonsonson claimed to have recorded the speed of dark and found it to be faster. He postulated that light was merely a very bright version of dark, which was in fact, the ultimate constant in the universe. Sonsonson pointed out that the vast majority of the universe is, in fact, dark and the only light is provided by big things on fire that are dotted here and there within the universal dark. Many established physicists suddenly became afraid of the dark, as it challenged the very basis of their beliefs and, more importantly, their research funding. They didn't relax until Sonsonson admitted the whole thing had merely been a highly technical advertising campaign to promote a rock band called The Dark. The band's only single, 'Dark the Hellish Angels Sing' managed to get to number forty-seven in the US charts but stayed at number one in Albania for fourteen years.

Ironically, Magnus Sonsonson's bogus Dark Theory was proved to be correct fifteen years later but by that time he had joined a Neo-New Age cult and moved to a bubble on Io where he changed his name to Tree Apostle Sunshine Bunny Wunny Shrub Fondler and spent his days ranting about the evils of kitchen appliances and formica.

The Big Suck

The Big Suck was the world's first upwards waterfall. Built as part of the Great Exhibition of 2253, the Big Suck used gravitic induction to send millions of tons of water flooding up the side of Mount Everest. Sadly, no one had anticipated that the water would freeze when it reached the top. Everest grew at an alarming rate until it pierced the ozone layer, causing a heat wave in Antarctica that confused no end of penguins.

Umbrellas

In order to avoid a soaking and the inevitable loincloth shrinkage caused by heavy rain, early man would shelter beneath the dense, leafy branches of a convenient tree during a downpour.

Naturally, this involved staying in one place for a period of time. A period of time in which a damp, pissed-off mammoth who didn't seem to suffer from shrinkage in the slightest, could turn up and gore you to avenge a previous spear-throwing incident. Modern elephants have inherited their 'never forget' appellation from the ancient mammoths, who, while being a tad shaky about the winners of the Grand National and members of FA cup final teams, always remembered the faces of every bastard that had ever thrown a spear at them.

Eventually, mankind theorized that standing around under trees when it was raining was not a good idea.

Especially if lightning was involved as well as mammoths. Hence the race was on to invent the umbrella. Early attempts consisted of a physically strong but mentally challenged individual ripping up a tree and carting it around on his shoulder in case of a downpour. Fortunately for the forests, this didn't catch on. The 'Sheltering under a mammoth' ploy showed early promise, but relied heavily on the mammoth remaining stationary during a rainstorm. Sadly, at the first sight of rain, a mammoth would stampede towards the nearest tree under which it could shelter, leaving behind a number of incredibly flat, wet Neanderthals who would have gone back to the drawing board if a) they could walk with every bone in their bodies broken and b) they'd invented the drawing board.

The umbrella was finally invented, but, ironically was initially used as a sunshade as befits its name which is derived from umbra – shade, and Ella – a lady of easy virtue who didn't like the sun. From the twentieth century onwards, umbrellas evolved into a unique form of currency in the western world. People would visit licensed premises with umbrellas, and leave them there. This abnegation of responsibility for possessions occurred for one of five reasons.

The individual involved:

1. Arrived when it was raining and left when it was dry, hence having no reminder of the need for an umbrella.
2. Became so drunk he or she forgot they had brought THEMSELF to the bar, let alone an umbrella.

3. Met a member of the opposite sex and lost interest in anything that didn't involve immediate, physical intimacy. (Only a very strange individual would include an umbrella in this category.)

4. Was a fanatical member of a defunct Eastern European death squad that used pointed umbrellas to inject lethal doses of the poison ricin into supposed political dissidents and didn't want to be caught with the murder weapon.

5. He or she forgot they had an umbrella with them. Although this might seem like a pathetic excuse, people do it all the time.

Whatever the reason, the loss of your umbrella immediately gives you the right to claim any other umbrella that you perceive to have been left behind by someone. The owner might have gone to the toilet, but, if they didn't take their umbrella with them ... it's yours. It's a karmic thing. Also, there's an element of sport involved. You should always claim an umbrella that is better than the one you mislayed. Otherwise you will be perceived as a sad loser, and people you thought you knew will spit on you in the street and curse your ancestors for passing on substandard, umbrella-related genes.

Few things are more exhilarating than spotting a good-looking brolly in the corner of a bar. A brolly that you know, in your heart of hearts, has been carelessly abandoned by its owner. You stalk this umbrella for hours on end, safe in the knowledge that it is far superior to the one you left in a taxi last week. You tease yourself with trips to the toilet and the elation you feel, as you return to see it, still standing there, is by no means better than sex. But it's better than nothing.

Finally, the bar has emptied. The barman is putting the chairs up on the tables and collecting the glasses. Your stamina has paid off. To the victor, the prize. You knock back the dregs of your drink with a cavalier toss of the head. You bid a cheery farewell to the barman, stride over, and grasp that which is rightfully yours. Then, as you march confidently towards the exit, the bouncer interposes his impressive bulk between you and the door and says 'Oi, where you goin' with my umbrella, you thievin' slag.'

At the end of the day, a little rain never hurt anybody.

Inventions and Sex

Throughout history, major inventions and sex have always been inextricably intertwined. I guarantee that the first wheeled vehicle ever produced was borrowed by the inventor's son, and used for a romantic liaison on the evening of its creation.

The creative urge and the sexual imperative have always been driving forces during mankind's development. It's little wonder they often became linked. I shan't bore you with the erotic possibilities of the Euclidean screw, or the sensual potential of the spinning jenny. Instead, I shall leap forth into a discourse on the relative merits of that most ubiquitous of grey, boxlike,

beeping things, the computer.

QUESTION: What is this universal infatuation with the Internet?

If someone had told me, a few years ago, that we'd be looking upon a phone conversation you had to type as a major innovation I'd have had them certified. And don't say 'But you can send pictures as well.' It takes about an hour to download a bloody picture, and half the time the tits are all out of focus ... oops. If I want to send someone a picture, I'll use a brand-new innovation called a stamp. Maybe I'm just getting old. However, there's something else that's really worrying me. I don't know if you've heard about it ... it's called DILDONICS. For anyone that isn't familiar with this term, it refers to the equipment they have in development at the moment, which will enable us to have sex with our computers. I don't know about you, but the only way I'm ever going to screw my computer is by plugging it in wrongly. I must confess, I am seriously worried about the whole concept of dildonics. It actually involves you putting your dick in a mechanical device that's linked to a computer. Are you sure? What happens if there's a power surge or a systems crash. It could rip your dick off and fax it to Canada before you know what's happening. No, thank you. I'll stick to the real thing. You know where you are with a good magazine.

How many people are surprised that the most popular sites on the Internet are pornographic? As I've already pointed out: every time someone comes up with a new invention, someone will immediately work out a way to get sex involved. As soon as the camera was invented, I can personally guarantee that the first film ever developed included at least two pictures of the inventor's girlfriend, naked. I can remember when polaroid cameras hit the shops. All right guys, what's the first thing you thought? 'You don't have to send the film to the chemist. They can be as saucy as you want.' It's pathetic but it's what we're like. It's a guy thing. I guarantee that if a guy invents invisibility at midday, he'll be in the ladies' showers at the local leisure centre by one o'clock.

This concept was demonstrated perfectly when Professor Blofish, prior to his dismissal from Imperial College, finally perfected his 'Spanner Scanner' – a device which allowed the events occurring in a previous time-span, in a given location, to be viewed again. Due to the limitations of the power supply at the time, the device could only replay events that had transpired during the last two milliseconds. This effectively allowed you to view anything that was happening, anywhere in the world, almost as it occured. Professor Blofish was forced to resign from the faculty when he was found alone, giggling and foaming at the mouth, viewing a female biochemistry student's room, by the Bursar. The Bursar immediately placed the equipment under lock and key and refused to release it for any reason whatsoever. Unless cash was involved. By a strange coincidence, I recently visited that very Bursar. A sum of money and a piece of equipment changed hands. I am now watching you read this book. Spooky, huh?

Life on a Liverpool housing estate left its mark on Craig Charles and provided the inspiration for his poetic social comment.

This talent led him to live performance of his work in the company of poets such as Roger McGough and Adrian Henri.

Some years later, tired of using his poetry as a vehicle for his sense of humour, Craig joined the alternative comedy circuit. This in turn led to appearances in many successful satirical radio and television programmes of the eighties, including *Loose Ends, Wogan* and *Saturday Night Live*, before he took on the role of Lister, the last remaining human being in BBC2's most successful ever sitcom, *Red Dwarf*.

His autobiography, *No Irish, No Niggers*, and his first collection of poetry, *No Other Blue*, are due to be published in 1998. Craig says 'Writing is the most fun you can have without wearing make-up!'.

Russell Bell's long list of talents includes playing as a session guitarist, scriptwriting, acting, stunt horse-riding, composing and producing music for film and advertising, and teaching Taekwondo. He has won major awards in most of these areas and is currently a full-time comedy writer.

READ MORE IN PENGUIN

In every corner of the world, on every subject under the sun, Penguin represents quality and variety – the very best in publishing today.

For complete information about books available from Penguin – including Puffins, Penguin Classics and Arkana – and how to order them, write to us at the appropriate address below. Please note that for copyright reasons the selection of books varies from country to country.

In the United Kingdom: Please write to *Dept. EP, Penguin Books Ltd, Bath Road, Harmondsworth, West Drayton, Middlesex UB7 ODA*

In the United States: Please write to *Consumer Sales, Penguin USA, P.O. Box 999, Dept. 17109, Bergenfield, New Jersey 07621-0120*. VISA and MasterCard holders call 1-800-253-6476 to order Penguin titles

In Canada: Please write to *Penguin Books Canada Ltd, 10 Alcorn Avenue, Suite 300, Toronto, Ontario M4V 3B2*

In Australia: Please write to *Penguin Books Australia Ltd, P.O. Box 257, Ringwood, Victoria 3134*

In New Zealand: Please write to *Penguin Books (NZ) Ltd, Private Bag 102902, North Shore Mail Centre, Auckland 10*

In India: Please write to *Penguin Books India Pvt Ltd, 706 Eros Apartments, 56 Nehru Place, New Delhi 110 019*

In the Netherlands: Please write to *Penguin Books Netherlands bv, Postbus 3507, NL-1001 AH Amsterdam*

In Germany: Please write to *Penguin Books Deutschland GmbH, Metzlerstrasse 26, 60594 Frankfurt am Main*

In Spain: Please write to *Penguin Books S. A., Bravo Murillo 19, 1° B, 28015 Madrid*

In Italy: Please write to *Penguin Italia s.r.l., Via Felice Casati 20, I–20124 Milano*

In France: Please write to *Penguin France S. A., 17 rue Lejeune, F–31000 Toulouse*

In Japan: Please write to *Penguin Books Japan, Ishikiribashi Building, 2–5–4, Suido, Bunkyo-ku, Tokyo 112*

In South Africa: Please write to *Longman Penguin Southern Africa (Pty) Ltd, Private Bag X08, Bertsham 2013*

READ MORE IN PENGUIN

Red Dwarf   Grant Naylor

When Lister got drunk, he got really drunk.

After celebrating his birthday with a Monopoly-board pub crawl around London, he came to in a burger bar on one of Saturn's moons, wearing a lady's pink Crimplene hat and a pair of yellow fishing waders, with no money and a passport in the name of 'Emily Berkenstein'.

Joining the Space Corps seemed a good idea. Red Dwarf, a clapped-out spaceship, was bound for Earth. It never made it, leaving Lister as the last remaining member of the human race, three million years from Earth, with only a dead man, a senile computer and a highly evolved cat for company.

They begin their journey home. On the way they'll break the Light Barrier. They'll meet Einstein, Archimedes, God and Norman Wisdom . . . and discover an alternative plane of Reality.

Better Than Life   Grant Naylor

Lister is lost. Three million years from Earth he's marooned in a world created by his own psyche. For Lister it's the most dangerous place he could possibly be because he's completely happy.

Rimmer has a problem too. He's dead. But that's not the problem. Rimmer's problem is that he's trapped in a landscape controlled by his own subconscious. And Rimmer's subconscious doesn't like him one little bit.

Together with Cat, the best-dressed entity in all six known universes, and Kryten, a sanitation Mechanoid with a missing sanity chip, they are trapped in the ultimate computer game: Better Than Life. The zenith of computer-game technology, BTL transports you directly to a perfect world of your imagination, a world where you can enjoy fabulous wealth and unmitigated success.

It's the ideal game – with only one drawback: it's so good, it'll kill you.

Also published in one volume as the **Red Dwarf Omnibus**

READ MORE IN PENGUIN

Last Human   Doug Naylor

Somewhere along the line, Lister had made a major mistake.

Why else would he find himself on a prison ship bound for Cyberia, the most inhospitable penal colony in Deep Space, sentenced to eighteen years' Hard Thought.

Dave Lister – the LAST HUMAN

The future of the species is in the hands of one man. And all he has to help him are his wits, his cunning, and a two-page girdle section from a mail-order catalogue.

'Smegging wonderful ... some of the comic riffs are sublime' – *Independent*

Backwards   Rob Grant

Dave Lister has finally found his way back to planet Earth. Which is good.

What's bad is that time isn't running in quite the right direction. And if he doesn't get off the planet soon, he's going to have to go through puberty again. Backwards.

Still, his crewmates have come to rescue him. Which is good.

Rejoin the trepid band of space zeroes from *Red Dwarf* and *Better Than Life* – Lister, Rimmer, Holly and the Cat – as they continue their epic journey through frontal-lobe-knotting realities where none dare venture but the bravest of the brave, the boldest of the bold, the feeblest of the feeble-minded.

READ MORE IN PENGUIN

Red Dwarf Quiz Book Sharon Burnett and Nicky Hooks

'This sounds like a twelve change of underwear trip!'

Gather yours together and prepare to launch into the ultimate *Red Dwarf* experience. Call yourself a fan? Can you remember: When is Gazpacho Soup Day? What is Space Corps Directive 196156? Who said, 'That's it, we're deader than tank tops!'? The *Red Dwarf Quiz Book* is bursting with tantalizing trivia and quirky questions. Enough to keep you amused for several thousand light years.

A Question of Smeg Sharon Burnett and Nicky Hooks
The Second Red Dwarf Quiz Book

Who taught foundation courses in Advanced Rebellion? Which character asked: 'How's life in hippy heaven you pregnant, baboon-bellied space beatnik?' And just who was Android 72264Y? You'll find these and many more in the All New *Red Dwarf* quiz book: a fun-filled volume full of teasing – and extremely DIFFICULT – questions based on the very latest *Red Dwarf* series and all four *Red Dwarf* novels. Oh, and ANSWERS, for those who get 'Lost'.

Primordial Soup Grant Naylor

Before recorded Time, there existed a substance known as Primordial Soup. From this disgustingly unpromising, gunky substance, all life began. Likewise, from the disgustingly unpromising, gunky scripts, sprang the disgusting, gunky comedy series, *Red Dwarf*.

Primordial Soup is a selection of the least worst scripts from the first five years of *Red Dwarf*, tracing the series from its humble beginnings to its humble present.

also published:

Son of Soup Rob Grant and Doug Naylor

The Log, *read by Craig Charles, is also available as a Penguin Audiobook.*